Chasing Santa

The Gumboot & Gumshoe Series: Book Five

Laura Hesse

Running L Productions

National Library of Canada Cataloguing in Publication Data Chasing Santa/by Laura Hesse
ISBN Print: 978-1-9990774-5-7 ISBN: E-Book 978-1-9990774-6-4
Cover Design: Autumn Sky, Self Pub Book Covers Inc. Publisher: Running L. Productions,
Vancouver Island, British Columbia, Canada
Website: www.Running L Productions.com

Contents

Foreword

The Gumboot & Gumshoe Series is a humorous entertaining cozy mysteries series set on the West Coast of Canada. While it helps if you have read the first four books in the series (Gumboots, Gumshoes and Murder, The Dastardly Mr. Deeds, Murder Most Fowl and Gertrude & The Sorcerer's Gold) to understand the characters and the world of Seal Island, this story is designed as a standalone.

Gumboots, Gumshoes and Murder was the first book in The Gumboot and Gumshoe Series followed by The Dastardly Mr. Deeds and Murder Most Fowl. These three novels need to be read in order.

Gertrude & The Sorcerer's Gold was inspired by actual events. Brother Twelve was a rogue prophet who during the 1920's began a journey that resulted in the formation of The Aquarian Society in 1927 in Nanaimo, British Columbia. He was the first spiritualist to welcome in the Age of Aquarius and even predicted the Stock Market Crash in the 1930's as well as World War II. He was also Canada's first cult leader. His hidden stash of gold coins has never been found.

The World of Seal Island

Seal Island is home to hippies, organic farmers, fishermen, billionaires, artists, and those wanting to escape the rat race. It is only accessible by ferry, float plane, or boat. The island residents like it that way. In the summer, the population swells a hundred-fold.

A colorful array of characters live or lived on the island including a moonshine making billionaire, a pot growing fisherman, a celebrity flower child, a sex addicted realtor, a womanizing pub owner, a down and out goat farmer, a 'special' boy who loves funny hats, a semi-retired supreme court judge, a pet psychic, a pack of Saint Bernard dogs, a cop, a pot-bellied pig, a Jersey cow, and a German shepherd afraid of crowds & loud noises.

Gertrude and Peaches, the pot-bellied pig and Jersey cow, are notorious for getting into trouble, leaving their mum, RCMP Sergeant Betty Bruce with a lot of mysteries to solve including the bizarre deaths of three friends in Gumboots, Gumshoes & Murder, solving the case of the real life mystery of the severed feet in sneakers that washed up on the coast of British Columbia, unraveling the case of the Painted Lady in The Dastardly Mister Deeds, bringing order to the island in Murder Most Fowl, and bringing the quest to find Brother Twelve's buried treasure to a supposed end in Gertrude & The Sorcerer's Gold.

Right, now for the conclusion to the Gumboot & Gumshoe Series

– Chasing Santa. Enjoy. Chasing Santa The Gumboot & Gumshoe Series: Book Four By Laura Hesse

Chasing Santa

The Santa Claus Blues

December 10th

A small skiff made its way to shore. Salt water sloshed against the little rowboat's sides as the man inside it, a jolly black-haired blue-eyed fellow dressed in a red velvet Santa suit, rowed as hard as he could against the out-going tide. Sweat beaded his brow. His breath was a frosty stream in front of his face. His cheeks were rosy from the cold.

Behind him an old catamaran rocked gently on its anchor, far enough out in the Strait of Georgia that it wouldn't end up marooned on the sand once the tide finished receding. Its sail was wrapped tightly against the main mast, the rigging still in the windless night. A solitary light glowed inside the round cabin windows below deck.

Stars twinkled overhead, the Milky Way a bedazzling display of flickering lights against the rolling frigid clouds of fog that drifted over the water.

The wiry man dressed as Santa Claus jumped out of the skiff, his black gumboots splashing in the surf as he tugged the boat onto shore. The dinghy's hull crunched on gravel.

In front of the Santa Claus thief stood a massive two-level cedar log home with an entertainment sized deck overlooking the strait. Patio bi-fold doors opened onto it. A stone fireplace and built-in gas barbecue walled in one side. Four cedar pillars held up the shake roof that covered the expanse.

The thief reached inside the velvet overcoat and pulled out a red hat and fake white beard. He donned the last of his costume and then fished a large garbage bag out from under the seat. The bag smelled faintly of fish.

With a grin on his face, he tugged on the black leather belly bag that held the tools of his trade, and with a spring in his step, walked across the beach to the house.

Christopher Nicholas thought it fitting that he assumed the role of Santa Claus at this time of year, given that he intended to liberate the rich of their burdens in order to aid the poor; namely, Christopher and his daughter, Sam.

Sam was the apple of his eye. She was a resilient kid. He thought himself one of the luckiest dad's in the world as he strode quickly across the deck and peered into the house.

Vaulted ceilings soared upwards. Wall to wall windows provided for breathtaking views. A plush white Italian leather sectional couch filled the living room. Original oil paintings of green forests and Haida carvings hung on the walls. Interspersed on the tables were glass vases filled with silver and gold Christmas balls. Fronds of plastic ivy wound its way up the staircase, red silk bows tied to each spindle. A tall imitation Christmas tree stood against one wall, its golden lights casting a soft glow around the room. There were already several Christmas presents wrapped in festive paper piled around the tree's base.

Chris grinned. It was the perfect score. He only wished he could afford a house like this. All he needed was another hundred grand and he could buy a two-bedroom house on the northern tip of the island. His daughter could go to school, maybe make some friends. He could get her a dog too. That would be fun. Sam would love that.

Chris walked over to the far side of the deck and leaned over a potted Japanese Maple.

He spotted what he was looking for, an alarm panel. It was on the wall beside the side door.

He tugged a pair of tiny opera glasses from his belly purse and examined the alarm.

"God bless these islanders," he grinned, noting that the alarm wasn't on. That meant the homeowners were home, asleep in their beds upstairs, thinking the cheap door locks were security enough.

Chris slipped quietly around the house to the side door and expertly popped the lock without difficulty.

Once inside, he took off his gumboots and left them by the door. He crept through the house, slinking upstairs, the murmur of velvet the only sound he made as he liberated the sleeping woman and man in the master bedroom of their jewelry. Chris noticed the small safe tucked away on a shelf behind some folded t-shirts in the walk-in closet right away and smothered a laugh.

He silently unscrewed the bolts that held it down, picked it up, and retreated down the stairs, placing the safe on the floor by the side door. It wasn't heavy, but its metal corners would slice through his loot bag.

Chris strolled into the kitchen and rifled through the cupboards. He found some boxes of sweet and salty popcorn and a bag of chocolate bars, plus a tin of honey roast peanuts. They all went into the big black garbage bag.

He then went to the fridge and pulled some chicken breasts and a frozen pizza out of the freezer. These along with three packs of grape juice, a head of lettuce, a carton of milk, a block of cheddar cheese, and two apples, also went into the bag.

Upon returning to the living room, the tall lanky man dressed as Santa Claus bent over and examined the presents under the tree, lifting each one and shaking it. The smaller presents looked like they might contain jewelry or some other expensive item. These went directly into the bag.

"Santa," a childlike voice gasped behind him, "you're early."

He spun around.

An impish three-year-old girl with big round eyes, a snotty nose, and wisps of curly blond hair, regarded him with wonder.

"Shhhh," he whispered, glancing down at the medium sized present in his hand. The name on the tag was Brittany. Chris quickly scanned the tags on the smaller presents inside the bag. The tags read to 'my wife'. That didn't help.

"Hey, you're supposed be asleep, Brittany," Chris continued, hoping he had the right name.

"You know me," she squeaked. "You are Santa."

"I am," the fraudulent Santa muttered, pulling a small red and white candy cane from his pocket and handing it to the child. This was his last one. He'd have to stock up again the next time he and Sam went shopping.

"Can you keep a secret?"

Brittany nodded, the picture of wide-eyed innocence.

"My elves made a mistake and mixed up the presents. I have to take these back to my workshop so we can deliver the right presents to the right Brittany," Chris lied. "Don't you worry, I'll be back with yours on Christmas."

"'Kay," she muttered, sucking on the candy cane.

"Off to bed now," he told her, resisting the urge to yell 'ho, ho, ho' lest he wake the child's parents.

Brittany grinned and ran upstairs.

Chris breathed a sigh of relief, put Brittany's present back under the tree, and bolted for the door. He slipped on his gumboots, picked up the safe, and ran back to the skiff carrying the safe under one arm like a football.

He tossed his bag of loot and the safe into the boat and pushed the skiff out into the water.

Chris smiled as he jumped in, and rowed with all his might, his back arching with every stroke of the oars, the outgoing tide helping the skiff along.

Brittany reminded him of Sam when she was that age, full of wonder and trust. That was before he lost his job, his house, and his marriage, in that order. The only thing he had hung onto was the catamaran he had salvaged and restored several years earlier. Sam never asked where her mommy was. That was a good thing. Stacey simply walked out one day so he packed up Sam, whatever he could fit onto the boat, and left, not sure what the future would hold only that so long as his daughter was with him, he would find a way.

**

Sam lay in her bunk inside one of the catamaran's pontoons

reading a tattered copy of *The Lion, The Witch, & The Wardrobe*. C. S. Lewis was her favorite author. She had ten dog-eared copies of his novels in the tiny hatch overhead.

Sam sighed wistfully and leaned over to stare wearily out the window at the faraway coastline. The orange glow from the streetlights in Comox and Courtenay looked creepy in the advancing fog.

Here and there, the house lights were popping on in the city and along the shore as people started their day.

A faint red line had appeared on the eastern horizon, the dawn chasing away the night like an orca hunting a seal.

The catamaran rocked gently on the water, almost lulling her to sleep. The small propane fueled heater in the cabin buzzed softly.

The winter was going to be colder than normal. She could sense it. The geese and trumpeter swans had long since flown south. They had gone early this year. Except for the seagulls, the other birds had also disappeared. The grey and white gulls huddled on shore, rarely following the catamaran like they usually did. She hadn't seen a humpback whale in ages.

Nine-year-old Samantha Nicholas grinned. Maybe it would snow for Christmas. That would be cool.

Oh, yeah, snow baby snow, she thought merrily.

A dull thud against the hull made her sit up.

Daddy was home.

She breathed a sigh of relief. There was always the chance that one day, he wouldn't.

Sam tugged on a plain grey cable-knit sweater and her running shoes and hurried up onto the deck. She flipped on the running lights as she did so.

She saw Santa Claus toss a bulky garbage bag onto the deck. A gunmetal grey safe followed that. The safe slid across the slippery deck before catching in some rope rigging. Santa climbed up the aluminum ladder onto the boat. His velvet suit drooped, saturated by both fog and seawater. He immediately hoisted the skiff out of the water and turned towards her.

"Hey, honey, what are you doing up," Santa Claus asked her patiently, clumping across the deck in his gumboots.

"Waiting for you," she smirked.

"Oh, sweetie, I told you to stop worrying so much," her daddy replied, playfully flipping her ponytail into the air.

Her father had already removed his hat and beard. His face was ruddy, his glacial blue eyes dancing with triumph.

Sam wrapped her arms around her body and shivered. It was bone chilling cold despite the giant woolen sweater that fell almost to her knees. Daddy looked happy. The caper must have gone well.

"Hey, go back inside," Chris commanded his daughter, concern replacing the penetrating stare he fired upon her.

"What's for breakfast," she asked, forcing a smile. She would give her right arm for Sugar Pops or Frosted Flakes.

"Pizza," her father declared proudly, pulling a frozen ham and pineapple pizza box out of his bag of swag.

"That's great, Daddy," she lied, hiding her disappointment. They ate pizza a lot.

"I've also got grape juice, chocolate bars, popcorn, and peanuts," he grinned. "After we move on and moor someplace for the day, maybe we can watch a movie on the VCR and pig out on junk food."

"Okay," Sam laughed. That was appealing. Hey, she was just a kid.

"Can we watch Free Willy?"

"Again," her father frowned.

Sam pursed her lips into her best pout ever, letting the bottom lip drop and quiver.

"Yeah, that doesn't work anymore," her father chortled. "Take 'the take' down below while I haul anchor."

"Yes, daddy," she agreed, dragging the weighty bag towards the hatch. "What's in here? The kitchen sink?"

"Lots of stuff," he responded. "Chicken, milk, lettuce, presents… oh, wait, did I just say presents?"

"Presents, huh," Sam's voice warbled.

Food, jewelry, coins, stuff like that was okay to steal by her way of thinking. Daddy said that was what insurance was for. Stealing somebody's Christmas gifts bothered Sam in a way that she couldn't quite put her finger on. She and her dad had been thieves for as long as she could remember. She went with him when he needed someone small to climb through a window to open a door. They had got the idea after watching the movie *Oliver*.

Wait! Did that mean her father was Fagan? He wasn't Bill Sykes. Daddy was too good a daddy.

Sam laughed lightly. She thought Fagan was a riot, even if he was a little hard on Oliver. He was funny, looked after the kids, and didn't have a wife either. Yep, Daddy was Fagan. Fagan would steal Christmas presents so she guessed that was just how it was.

Did she want her dad to stop stealing? No.

She loved the prettily wrapped presents that appeared in her stocking on Christmas morning even if they were supposed to be someone else's. Besides, her daddy didn't work Christmas eve or Christmas day.

Once, her father had mistakenly given her a very expensive pearl necklace. Another Christmas, she got a Cuban cigar and a toy hand grenade. Her father had almost fainted when she pulled the weirdly wrapped tiny football out of her stocking and unwrapped it. Surprise! Daddy ripped it out of her hand and tossed it overboard, so she wasn't quite sure about that one.

"Don't worry," Santa-daddy replied. "I didn't take Brittany's."

"Who is Brittany," she shouted from inside the galley.

"Later," her father yelled back.

Instantly, Sam heard the scrape of the anchor as her father hauled it aboard. The boat skipped sideways, caught in the current. The catamaran tended to surf the waves rather than tilt sideways like a regular sailboat, the two pontoons providing incredible stability.

Sam began unloading the food out of the garbage bag and tucking the chicken, milk and juice away in the small fridge in the galley, and the dry goods into the cupboards. She unwrapped the pizza and popped it into the microwave.

Her father started the twin engines. The two small diesels sputtered into life and the catamaran glided smoothly over the salt water as her father guided the boat into the middle of the strait. There wasn't enough wind to use the sails.

Drop anchor, do a job, hoist anchor, and find a deserted cove to see what they got, rest and repeat. That was the Nicholas family's life.

Sam thought it was a glorious life, imagining her daddy as Blackbeard and she as his first mate, feared pirates of the high seas. Women would swoon over her father. Men would run in fear.

She thought the thirty-eight-foot catamaran was aptly named for pirating. Her father had christened it *Polar Bear Express* when he re-built the boat from the fiberglass hull up, skimping only on the quality of the interior, which he bought from Ikea and later customized.

Sam leapt forward, one arm raised over her head, legs bent in a sword fighter's stance, her lips pursed into a thin line, her brows knitting together as she plunged a butter knife into the empty pizza box like a sword: the famed Nicholas' were here! Pirates of the high seas. Pillagers of the West Coast.

Sam backed up and saluted the torn pizza box with the butter knife.

Once a month they would go to Vancouver to see Uncle Harry to cash in. Uncle Harry wasn't her real uncle, but he was always nice and had a special gift just for her. Usually it was food. His lamb kabobs and cinnamon buns were the bomb.

Life was good.

What kid her age could helm a boat, go to sleep listening to whale song, laugh at the dolphins playing in the catamaran's wake, and eagle watch to her heart's content. And then there were the spirit bears. Her father had taken her to see the sacred white Kermode bears when she was only four. It was the trip of a lifetime and they had done it not once, not twice, but ten times already. Okay, she counted on her fingers, that was ten trips of a lifetime.

Yep, being a thief's daughter wasn't all that bad, especially when your daddy was Santa Claus.

On Weddings & Pirate Treasure

December 11th - morning

The church bells rang as Betty Bruce and Reggie Phoenix stepped onto the dew-covered steps of the picturesque, weathered church that sat at the top of the hill overlooking the landing on Seal Island.

The sun broke out of the clouds as if on cue. It wouldn't reach its zenith for another hour. The couple had decided upon an early wedding, so they had time to get a good head start in *The Persephone*, Reggie's reconstructed fishing trawler, towards their honeymoon destination of Haida Gwaii and beyond.

Betty wore an ivory wedding dress that hugged her voluptuous figure, her shoulder length silver blond hair tucked above her head, held in place by antique herring bone pins. She wore little makeup as she was a commanding woman, made even more striking by the blush in her cheeks and warmth of her smile. She wasn't a beautiful woman, but she was handsome, and today, on her wedding day, she glowed with an internal fire that set many a mature man's heart to racing.

The groom was a giant of a man. He wore a grey tuxedo jacket over a navy-blue sweater. His slacks were black with crisp lines at the front. His tussle of curly grey locks and grey beard were neatly trimmed. The laugh lines etched deeply into his face spoke volumes as to his easygoing and caring nature.

One of the incongruous items the handsome couple wore was on their feet. Instead of high heels, Betty wore her knee-high regulation RCMP brown leather boots. The toes poked out from beneath the lacey hem of her wedding dress. Reggie, as always, wore thick soled black gumboots.

The other oddity was the rotund grey and white pot-bellied pig with a leather halter around her ample girth, a quizzical look on her face as she stood munching on one of the flower arrangements that had been attached to the end of a church pew. The bride's father, a dapper silver-foxed tuxedo clad man held onto the pig's halter.

Archie Bruce led Gertrude, the pot-bellied pig, out of the church. Violet Bone, a tiny, wizened woman wearing an emerald green wool dress and a forest green wool cloak joined him. A black and sable German shepherd walked beside her.

The sizeable crowd of fishermen, local farmers, and members of the Seal Island Vagabond Writer's Association, mostly women, gathered outside the church, also wearing gumboots. On Seal Island, the weather could change in an instant and rain was in the forecast.

Off to one side, a chestnut-haired farmer stood beside his wife, a dreadlocked woman wearing a colorful handwoven cloak and skirt, holding a lead rope. At the end of the lead rope stood a disgruntled peach colored Jersey cow.

The pastor had steadfastly refused to allow the pot-bellied pig and the Jersey cow into the church together, such was their reputation for mischief. Gertrude alone was a force to be reckoned with. Betty and Reggie had conceded that hauling Peaches into the church was a bit much to ask.

As one, the group of celebrants cheered heartily as Betty and Reggie slowly descended the steps.

Reggie grinned like the Cheshire cat. Betty laughed lightly and kissed Reggie on the cheek.

The crowd erupted into ever louder cheers.

The pig's hooves scrabbled on the stairs as it stepped down, its great belly rubbing against each one.

"There she blows," a fisherman yelled as Gertrude slipped down the last two steps, hauling the old man along with her.

"Dad!" Betty yelped, spinning around on her heels.

"Hang on, Arch," Reggie hollered, rushing to the rescue.

Archie let of of Gertrude's leash and grabbed for Reggie's outstretched hand. Reggie folded his big mitt around the wiry old man's age spotted one and steadied his teetering form, pushing him backwards lest Archie cartwheel the rest of the way down.

The German shepherd whined and wagged its tail, looking from its handler to Betty and then back again, as if asking what to do. The petite woman in green rested a comforting hand on the dog's shoulder, the other hand flying to cover her mouth as she cringed in fear, worried for her boyfriend, Archie.

Betty sighed with relief and wrapped her arms around her father once Reggie stepped away.

"That was a close one," Archie grinned. "You know what George Burns used to say. The secret to a long life is not to fall."

More of the bridal party exited the church including two senior widows, a roguish cherub faced young man in a felt top hat and antique waist coat, a flame-haired gangly goat farmer and his twin sister, a broad shouldered crewcut Adonis, a long haired vivacious blond, and several other young men and women who worked for the groom.

Pastor Brown closed the church doors behind him as the last of the group gathered in front of the church.

"Not locking the doors yet, are ya father," Reggie called to the pastor. "We might like ta get some more photos in the church."

"Just want to keep the heat in, is all," the pastor stuttered.

"You mean you want to keep Gertie out," a man in the crowd shouted.

"That too," the pastor replied guiltily.

Everyone laughed.

"Bet she ate the flowers right off the sides of the pews," a bleary-eyed member of the writer's society joked, angry at not being able to attend the service because the church was too small to hold everyone.

"Within the first five minutes, Dottie," Archie laughed.

"She had a little help from Champ too, I'm afraid," Violet chortled. The retired Supreme Court judge stroked the shepherd's head. The dog wagged its tail.

Betty and Reggie posed alongside the pot-bellied pig, Jersey cow, and German shepherd for pictures. The critters were family, after all, and local celebrities.

"Come on, Arch, sidle up to your daughter," Morris Tweedsmuir, the gangly goat farmer said, motioning Archie to stand in beside the happy couple.

"I don't think there's room," Archie joked.

"You too, Vi," Alana Tweedsmuir ordered Violet.

"Oh, I don't think so," Vi twittered.

"Come on, Vi, in ya come," Reggie cajoled her.

Archie wrapped an arm around her shoulder and urged her forward.

Cell phones clicked. Cameras whirred.

"Definitely a keeper," the handsome detective, Ben Hammerton, crooned, leaning over Alana's shoulder to look at the picture she just snapped with her ipad. The couple had been inseparable since Gertrude had unearthed Brother Twelve's missing stash of gold coins, solving an almost one-hundred-year-old mystery. "The guys at Head Office are going to love that one."

"Yep, you don't see this every day," Alana chuckled. "Too bad Betty couldn't wear her red serge RCMP dress uniform to get married in."

"Not going there," Betty laughed. "I am officially and completely retired."

"Only until your needed," Ben kidded her.

Betty and many locals had started off on the wrong foot with the young detective, when Ben had nearly killed Peaches, the Jersey cow, by tasering it instead of the pig who was on the run with a severed foot in her mouth. An angry mob of farmers and fishermen had tried to lynch him, but Betty had intervened. Alana was a good influence. The same men who wanted to hang him now stood shoulder to shoulder beside him at the wedding.

"Oh, you look so beautiful, Betty," Rainbow McDonald, the hippy teamaker and herb grower, gushed as she stood beside her husband Frank. The pair sometimes took care of Gertrude and Peaches when Betty and Reggie were away on the boat.

"That's so sweet, thank-you," Betty beamed, rubbing Peaches

nose.

"So, are you going to change your last name to Phoenix," eighty-nine-year-old Pearl Tullis asked her, a gleam in her sky-blue eyes. Pearl could finally see now that her cataracts were gone.

"I told her that she doesn't have ta, Pearl," Reggie drawled. "I'm an enlightened man, don't ya know."

A few of the men guffawed.

"I am and I dare anyone here to say otherwise," Reggie growled, hands on his hips.

"How about we answer that question down at the pub," Betty chuckled, slipping an arm under her husband's. "With a pint or two."

"Yer right, Bets, this getting married thing is thirsty business," the groom grinned.

"It's twelve o'clock somewhere," Betty chimed.

A loud 'hooray' went up as the bride, groom, pig, cow, dog, and friends and family escorted the couple down the hill to the Bristling Boar Pub where the owner and his staff had prepared a buffet luncheon for island residents only in celebration of Betty and Reggie's tying the knot.

***

The barrel-chested pub owner looked over the buffet table in all its glory. The kitchen staff had outdone themselves. There was smoked salmon, roast beef, ham, garlic prawns, oysters, and so much more. He had gone all out for his poker buddy's wedding. Given the corners he had cut to keep the pub afloat after paying a generous lawyer's bill, he couldn't fault the re-tired RMCP Sergeant and very special agent, Betty Bruce, either. He wasn't singing the jailbird blues, even though his wife and brother were.

Stew Mann turned towards the bar when he saw the crowd advancing down the hill, Reggie and Betty leading the way.

"Places everyone, here they come," he shouted to his staff. "Peggy, start pouring draft."

The stubby torpedo-bosomed bartender shot him a thumb's up and started pouring glasses of draft, readying herself for the onslaught.

Stew realized Gertrude had made a breakaway, making a bee-line for the pub's front door.

"Oh, no, you don't, Gertie," Stew screamed, racing to the front door and bolting it closed. "You are not taking down that buffet table."

"I'll get Harold," Peggy shouted in alarm. "I think he put a platter together for the critters."

When Peaches realized that Gertrude was well ahead of her, the cow leapt into the air, tugging the lead rope from Frank McDonald's hands, and bolted after her friend.

The whole wedding party sprinted after the pig and cow. The bride and groom raced after them, knowing the disaster that would ensue if the pig broke into the pub. Archie and Violet stayed behind, walking nonchalantly on, laughing raucously.

Stew put his shoulder against the door as the pig barreled up the stairs and head butted the door, the cow sliding to a stop at the base of the entrance. Peaches didn't like stairs.

The glass door rattled and shook. Pig spit slimed the once pristine glass.

"Oh no, Gertie, not today," he seethed.

The pub's head cook, a harried Native man, jogged out of the kitchen carrying two large salad bowls of vegetable ends. He stopped beside his boss.

"What's the plan," Walter gasped.

"We wait for Betty and Reggie to haul Gertie away from the door and then you slip the bowls out," Stew hissed. "That should keep Gert busy for a while."

"They're pretty big bowls," Walter grimaced. "You're going to have to open them real wide. Won't she break in?"

Gertie rammed the door, her nostrils quivering as the scent of the buffet drifted out from under the door.

"I ain't ever seen Gertie this aggressive before," Stew moaned.

"Maybe they forgot to feed her breakfast in all the bustle of the wedding preparations," Walter suggested.

"You might be right," Stew admitted. "That would explain it."

The bride and groom vaulted up the stairs two at a time. Betty snatched up the leather leash, but the pig was too strong for her. Reggie threw himself on top of Gertrude and tried to wrestle her away from the door, but the pig wouldn't budge.

"There's no way I'm opening this door," Stew shouted.

"Why don't you go out the kitchen door, Walter," Peggy hollered from behind them as Gertrude body slammed Reggie. The entire building shook from the impact. "Take the food bowls out front."

"Gertrude, you're a naughty pig," Betty wailed as her father ran up onto the porch to help.

"Good idea, Peg," Stew huffed, leaning harder into the door so that the lock and doorframe wouldn't shatter. Even though Stew was built like a linebacker, the pig outweighed him by fifty pounds or more. "Go around back."

Walter nodded and ran back into the kitchen.

It only took a minute for him to get around the front of the building.

The crowd saw him and cheered raucously, shouting encouragement.

"Here, Peaches. Here, cow," Walter shouted over the din. He put one of the food bowls down on the ground. The cow turned her head towards him, mooed, and jogged over to the salad bowl. She stuffed her nose into the bowl, snafued a carrot out of the mix and happily crunched away.

Gertrude stopped short, her nostrils quivering, her head swiveling around. She peered under the porch railing.

"Here, Gertie," Walter crooned, expertly flipping the salad in the second bowl.

Gertrude squealed, barged past Betty, and knocked Reggie onto his buttocks. Archie jumped out of the way just in time. One close call was enough for him.

The pig waddled down the steps and over to the metal salad bowl.

"Hooray," Stew sang as he opened the pub door to let everyone in.

Betty roared with laughter and helped her embarrassed husband to his feet. He grinned and wrapped an arm around her. He gave her a quick peck on the cheek before striding alongside his wife into the pub.

"I am so glad I don't have to deal with that pig every day," Ben whispered to Alana as they followed the crowd into the pub. She laughed lightly and punched him on the arm.

"Ah, but she's famous, don't you know," Alana mumbled back within earshot of Stew.

"Yeah, but not in a good way," Stew Mann chortled as the pair of lovebirds waltzed by him.

Stew waited for the last of the old ladies, Ida Abercrombie, and her nephew, Russell 'Also' Russell, wearing a black felt top hat and old-fashioned topcoat and tails, to enter the pub and then closed and locked the doors. For this one time only, he allowed the German shepherd to come in since the dog was well behaved and had already settled under the head table at Betty's feet.

Screw the health inspectors, he thought.

The till went 'ka-ching' and Stew's day got even brighter.

He cast one last glance out the window at the pig and cow before heading back to the bar to help Peggy and his staff deliver a round of drinks to everyone. He was covering the cost of the first round of beers as a wedding gift to his best buddy, but after that it was all profit.

In the distance, he saw a catamaran under full sail skipping along the strait, heading south by south-east around the point. The boat was travelling at a good clip as it skimmed over the top of the water like a kingfisher.

**

Sam leaned forward in the vinyl captain's chair. She was at the helm while her father sat at the outside table with a hand drill trying to open the safe. It had proven a stubborn little thing. He had been working at it since yesterday.

The take from the robbery yesterday was a good one, and he was pleased. While the jewelry from the master bedroom was mostly diamante pins and broaches, the four square smaller boxes from under the Christmas tree had yielded a matching emerald lady's ring and earrings, a men's diamond studded ring, and an antique emerald and diamond broach that daddy thought was worth at least ten thousand dollars for the broach alone.

She had asked her father if she could keep the small gold unicorn pendant that was part of the jewelry box haul. She wore it around her neck under her sweater.

The sound of the drill biting into the safe's metal locking mechanism was sharp. It bit through the whine of the wind and snap of the mainsail.

Sam reveled in the feel of the ship's wheel in her hands, at the power beneath her fingertips. She glanced at the gauges; she was keeping the *Polar Bear Express* steady at nine knots. The boat skimmed across the water like the sleek beauty that it was.

They were just rounding the southernmost tip of Seal Island when she trimmed the sails and slowed down to seven knots. A group of sea lions slept on the rocks by the lighthouse on the point. The giant bull seals raised their heads and stared at them as they cruised by.

Seagulls trailed along beside them.

Sam grinned. It was a glorious day.

"Yes," Chris shouted, finally breaking the lock on the safe.

Sam glanced over at her father as he rifled through the contents of the safe.

"Damn it," he swore. "It's just legal papers."

"Are you sure," Sam cautioned him. In their haste to toss out some useless papers once, they had almost missed some cashable bonds. "What about that big white envelope? That doesn't look like something legal papers would be in."

"Nah," her father scowled, opening the nine by eleven-inch envelope. "It's just copies of passport documents."

"What about the passports," Sam asked. "Can we sell those?"

"Maybe," he shrugged. "I'll ask your uncle."

"Well, it wasn't a total bust," Sam consoled him, slowing the catamaran even more.

"Yeah, the jewelry will fetch us a good price," he smiled, standing up and stretching.

Chris tossed the safe overboard. He then stuffed the legal papers into a metal container, poured a squirt of lighter fluid on it, and lit the papers on fire. He tucked the passports in the back pocket of his jeans.

Sam's nose wrinkled as the papers burned.

"So, how's it going, Captain," he asked his daughter, leaning against the railing and examining the cottages they passed by. The weather worn cottages didn't look ritzy enough to be worth breaking into. In most cases, they were atop high cliffs which wouldn't do.

"There's a nice-looking cove around the point," Sam nodded towards the charts in front of her. "I thought we could check it out and see if it's a good place to lie low for a day or two."

"This is Seal Island, isn't it," he glanced over his shoulder at her.

She nodded.

"Who knows, maybe we can search for treasure while we're there."

"What kind of treasure," Sam asked, her eyes lighting up.

"I heard tell that a pot-bellied pig unearthed some gold coins," he grinned as the gleam in his daughter's eyes grew brighter. "Maybe there's more."

"Really?"

"Really," he agreed.

The catamaran soared past a rocky cliff. The rocky cliff gave way to a rock-strewn beach, the rocks getting smaller and smaller as they approached the horseshoe shaped curve on the north-eastern tip of the island. A red barn and log cottage were visible in the inlet. Watchtower Mountain rose high into the distance, the top broken off as if God had chopped it off with a machete.

"That must be the cove you were talking about," Chris pointed.

"I didn't realize it would be so close to that farm," Sam worried, biting her lip.

"It's not as private as we like, but we're going treasure hunting, not casing the joint," Chris teased her. "Think we can pretend to be tourists for a day or two?"

"Oh, yeah," Sam beamed.

"Then take her in, Captain," Chris motioned towards the cove.

Sam's brow knitted together in concentration as she approached the cove at five knots. At the last minute, she let the jib ruff so that the wind caught the sail at an angle, while she spun the wheel to turn the boat ninety degrees to slide the bow around to face the cove. The sails flapped as they lost the wind and the boat slowed.

Chris leaned over and gave his daughter a hug.

"Couldn't have done it better myself," the proud father gloated.

"Drop the anchor, first mate," she ordered her father.

"Aye, aye, sir," he said crisply, snapping a salute.

Sam returned the salute, fidgeting in the captain's chair, vibrating at the thought of a real live treasure hunt. She didn't know why there were gold coins buried on this island but digging for them sounded like fun.

She didn't realize when she picked that cove that she was close to the exact spot where Brother Twelve's old cabin sat within the trees, hidden from view, the hole where Gertrude had found the wooden crate with mason jars filled to the brim with double eagle gold coins excavated to epic proportions as others sought to find more of British Columbia's false prophet's ill-gotten gains.

Her stomach growled. Lunch was in order. Her hunger pushed all thoughts of treasure aside.

While her father set anchor and battened down the main sail, Sam stepped down from the fly bridge and entered the top cabin. She grabbed a jar of peanut butter and raspberry jam from the cupboard and started making peanut butter and jam sandwiches for two. If daddy and she were going to go treasure hunting, they would need energy.

Cast On, Cast Off

December 11th – late afternoon

The wedding guests lined the dock. Reggie offered his hand to Betty as she climbed aboard *The Persephone*, the thirty-five-foot trawler that Reggie had converted into a dive and pot smuggling boat. Reggie was on the straight and narrow now, having gone legitimate, licensing his specialized cannabis lines to a multi-national corporation.

"Heave to, mate," a fisherman joked, loosening the trawler's lines.

"More like heave ho," another man added, unfastening the last of the mooring lines as Reggie boarded his vessel.

Reggie wagged a warning finger in their direction. Both men grinned.

"Take care of my daughter, you scoundrel," Archie kidded his son-in-law.

"Or you'll have us to answer to," Vi joined in.

Betty's German shepherd, a retired drug-sniffing dog, leapt over the railing onto the wood stained deck in a single bound. Champ barked with happiness, glad to be free of the crowd. Though much better than he was when he came to Seal Island, the shepherd still tended to hang his tail and hunch his shoulders when surrounded by too many people.

"Stay out of trouble, Hammerton," Betty shouted to the blond-haired detective helping with the mooring lines.

For all his muscles, Ben nearly lost his footing, catching his balance at the last minute before taking a dive into the frigid waters.

The two fishermen beside him laughed and slapped him

heartily on the back, once more sending him careening towards the wharf's edge. Alana raced forward and yanked her boyfriend backwards. They toppled on top of each other on the wooden dock.

"Apparently, I can't guarantee that," Hammerton hollered from beneath Alana.

"Definitely not," Alana giggled, extricating herself from Ben.

The men cheered, the ladies clapping enthusiastically, as Reggie swept his bride into his arms and carried her over the threshold into the cabin.

Betty blushed as she waved to her friends and neighbors.

Reggie placed her gently down, kissed her warmly, and then started up the diesel engine. Blue smoke coughed out the back of the boat, sending those still gathered on the docks scurrying back to the pub.

As the black hulled wooden trawler with fire engine red trim pulled away from the dock, the German shepherd stood sentry, wagging its tail furiously.

Betty watched out the window as Frank and Rainbow escorted Gertrude and Peaches up North Shore Road, walking hand in hand, the pig's leash in Frank's other hand and Peaches lead line in Rainbow's. Every few paces, Frank had to let go of his wife to urge Gertrude forward by dangling a Milk Bone in front of her snout.

Betty grinned. The animals were in good hands.

"We didn't miss anything, did we, Mr Phoenix," she asked her husband.

"If we did, there are plenty of places we can stop along the way, Mrs Phoenix," he beamed, his face breaking into a boyish grin.

Betty's heart swelled, heat rising into her cheeks. The love she felt for the man at the helm was endless. It had taken her thirty-five years to find the man of her dreams, even though he was right in front of her nose the whole time.

The last three years had been eventful, filled with heartbreak and joy, betrayal and redemption. Two murders, a friend's bizarre death, and a tragic drowning, had all been solved, plus she had unraveled the mystery behind the severed feet, and helped unearth a fortune in gold coins. She had lost one love only to find another and in doing so, left the pain caused by an abusive marriage behind.

Betty was tired of the limelight. Though not seeking it out, it always seemed to find her. The needs of others had forced her to compartmentalize her life and her feelings. Now she was free. Her RCMP pension provided enough income to live comfortably, plus the odd contract job as Special Consultant to the RCMP added to her bank account. Reggie had hired Melanie to manage the greenhouses and was taking some much-needed time to off from his business.

Champ, Betty's law enforcement partner, had taken to life at sea like his name implied.

The only thing still in question was whether they would continue to live in the house that Andy, her previous boyfriend, had left her. It was a beautiful Cape Cod on a stunning acreage in the shadow of Watchtower Mountain. It had a wonderful four stall barn where Peaches and Gertrude lived when Betty has at home. Betty loved it there, but her marriage to Reggie changed all that.

While Reggie never complained, she realized he must feel odd sleeping in the same bed that Betty had shared with her lover, the hot romance writer, Andy McDowell.

Andy's memory was fading now, but he would always have a place in her heart. She still placed flowers on his grave. He had no other family but her. Betty did that for Tiffany Hyde-White and Summer River too; although Tiffany's parents came a couple of times a year to visit their daughter.

"Penny for yer thoughts," Reggie rumbled as *The Persephone* chugged past Violet Bone's cedar A-frame home on top of the cliff facing northwest towards Vancouver Island.

Andy had died at the base of that cliff, below the cottage. Betty inhaled sharply. She prayed that his ghost was at peace. Maybe when they got back from her honeymoon, she would ask Rainbow, the pet psychic, if she could sense anything.

"I was thinking how lucky I am," Betty whispered, leaning

against Reggie's shoulder, forcing the dark thoughts away. "I also want to get out of this dress. The lace is making me itch."

"Well, I could drop anchor and help ya with both," he offered, a gleam in his eye.

"That sounds nice, but I'd rather wait until we get farther up island for that," she grinned.

"You're the boss," he chuckled.

"I'm going to change and put on a fresh pot of coffee," she added, pulling away. "I'm still a bit tipsy from brunch."

"Aye, that sounds good," he agreed. "I could use a cup a java too."

Betty planted a wet kiss on his cheek. He tilted his head and drew her lips closer to his, kissing her passionately.

She broke away breathless.

"Now ya can go get out of that dress," he crooned, turning back to the helm as a couple of trawlers pulled up beside him and blew their horns.

Betty laughed, hiked up her skirt, and clomped down the stairs into the cabin as Reggie picked up the radio and thanked the captains for the sendoff.

Champ barked furiously as he raced back and forth across the deck.

"Are we going to stop in Desolation Sound tonight," Betty yelled once she couldn't hear Reggie on the radio anymore.

She wriggled out of the wedding dress and slipped a teal shirt over her head, followed by a blue woolen Guernsey sweater. After tugging off her leather boots, she climbed into her jeans.

"Think so, weather permitting," Reggie shouted back. "Bill said it is coming down fierce in Powell River. They just posted a high wind warning."

Betty poked her head up through the galley hatch.

"That doesn't sound good."

"That's what we get for tying the knot in December," he shrugged.

"Why don't we park in Tribune Bay," Betty suggested. "That's as good a place to honeymoon as any."

"We don't park *The Persephone*, honey," Reggie grimaced. "We moor her."

"Moor, schmoor, I'll start the coffee," she smirked, ducking back below deck.

"Benny Lee captains the *Salty Dawg*. He was one of the chaps that honked us," Reggie continued, focused on piloting the boat. "Benny told me this strange story about some guy dressed as Santa Claus breaking into houses in Courtenay. He says he got us a wedding gift. It's a parrot."

"A parrot? What're we going to do with a parrot?"

"Depends on the parrot," Reggie mused aloud.

"I heard that," she laughed, spooning coffee into the coffee maker.

"I once saw a stripper whose parrot helped her peel," Reggie drawled. "Maybe before we say 'no', we should find out more about it."

"In your dreams," Betty guffawed.

"Probably for a long time," her husband mumbled.

"I heard that too," Betty snorted, climbing out of the galley.

Reggie cast an amused look her way.

"You figure he's doing it by sea," Betty said, changing the subject. "The Santa Claus thief, I mean, not the peeler's parrot."

"Would make sense," Reggie grinned.

"So, we have to be on the lookout for a Santa Claus driving a boat," she replied, as straight faced as she could.

"Nope, we're just gonna wave if we see jolly old Saint Nick on the high seas," he smirked. "Trust me, there's a lot of them at this time of year and…"

"And…," Betty queried.

"And we've got better things ta do," Reggie whispered huskily.

"We do that," she murmured, leaning in for another kiss.

"Hornby Island, it is," he replied eagerly, pulling away, his cheeks as rosy as Betty's own.

"How long until we get there?"

"Not soon enough," he said, laying on the throttle.

The dog bounced into the cabin and wiggled in between the

two of them, looking for some loving.

Betty and Reggie laughed merrily.

Along the mainland to the north, a spectacular array of angry black clouds had gathered over the mountains. The waves rose higher and higher as the north wind barreled down the coast. Whitecaps grew longer and wilder as the first of many winter storms rolled in.

Betty leaned over and kissed the dog between the ears, then moved to stand behind her husband, wrapping her arms around his waist, a Mona Lisa smile on her lips.

***

Chris rowed himself and his daughter to shore in the light skiff. They pulled it up onto the beach, tucked the oars under the seat, and looked around.

"It looks too rocky to go that way," Sam said, pointing at the large rock outcropping on the point.

"That leaves this-away," Chris replied.

Sam grinned and took hold of her father's hand. They walked along the sandy beach towards the forest.

"That looks like a trail," Sam cried, skipping ahead of her father.

Chris swayed slightly as he walked, taking a little longer than his daughter to get his land legs.

"Don't go too far without me," he warned her as she disappeared into the forest.

"I won't," Sam yelled back.

Chris picked up his pace. It was a nice day for December, not raining yet, although the clouds on the horizon forecast something different.

"Sam," he hollered, stepping onto the in-land trail. He didn't like losing sight of his daughter. From what he'd heard about Seal Island on the news, it could be a dodgy kind of place, what with buried treasure, strange deaths, and other odd bits he had heard tales of along the way. In hindsight, maybe they shouldn't have stopped here. Panic instantly rose inside his breast when

Sam didn't answer.

Chris bolted up the trail.

"SAM!"

"Over here," her faint voice drifted through the trees.

Chris raced on, jumping over stumps and debris. He broke into a clearing and saw the sod-roofed cabin, its door wide open to the elements, the broken windows covered in a tattered layer of plastic. His daughter stood in the doorway, looking in.

"This place is really cool," Sam grinned. "Stinky though."

"Be careful. It's probably not safe," he scolded her.

"Oh, Daddy," she replied, ignoring him and entering the cabin.

"Sam, get out of there!"

"It's all right," she re-emerged from Brother Twelve's former home. "There's nothing in here but a broken bed and table plus some rusty tin cans."

"Listen to me when I tell you something, young lady," Chris fumed.

"Yes, sir," she replied, contrite.

"Come on, let's follow the trail and see where it leads," Chris said, play punching her in the arm. He didn't want to ruin their day, but a gloomy sense of foreboding had settled over him.

"This old hut gives me the willies," he murmured, but his daughter simply grinned and raced off, ponytail bouncing.

He strolled after her, inhaling, exhaling, calming his suddenly jittery nerves.

A scream echoed through the woods as her bobbing head suddenly disappeared beneath from view as if the earth had swallowed her whole.

"SAM!"

Chris raced to his daughter, his heart pounding.

"Daddy, stop," Sam hollered.

Chris stumbled to a stop, grabbing at a bush to keep from falling into the deep hole his daughter sat at the bottom of. He jumped down and knelt beside her, checking her outstretched leg for broken bones.

"I'm okay," she moaned, slapping her father's hands away.

"Next time, not so fast on an unknown trail. Right," he ruffled her hair.

"Right," she groaned, extricating herself from the gravel at the bottom of the wide hole.

Chris helped his daughter climb back out, and they stood together, looking around at the myriad of holes dug into the forest floor. Some holes were small, others massive excavations like the one that Sam had fallen into.

"You think this is where they unearthed that treasure," his daughter asked him.

"I think so," he replied, stupefied.

"Wow!"

"Wow is the word," he muttered, his eyes widening. It was true. Someone had found buried treasure on Seal Island. Chris hadn't really believed the story, but here was the evidence, right in front of his eyes. This changed everything.

"You think the guy who lived in the cabin buried the treasure," Sam queried, pointing towards the sod hut.

"Possibly," Chris agreed. "I heard tell the guy was some kind of prophet in the 1920's who headed up a doomsday cult. He stole his members money and amassed a fortune, turning it into gold coins and burying it on islands up and down the coast."

"That's cool," Sam gasped, awestruck.

"Not for the folks that believed in him."

The wind picked up, the weather starting to turn. Tree branches tapped against each other, the tops of the trees swaying slightly.

"Maybe we should we head home," Sam suggested.

"It's not raining yet," he said, noticing what looked like a road ahead of them. "Let's keep going for a while."

Sam was off once again, dodging around the edges of the pits, heading towards the opening that heralded the roundabout at the end of South Shore Road.

Chris cased the cottages they passed, most not worthy of a second glance. He doubted there would be much to steal.

Father and daughter stopped at a quaint cedar bungalow.

Brambles had overtaken the yard, but the house looked well kept. The door and window frames sported a fresh coat of paint - robin's egg blue. The color looked nice against the weathered cedar siding.

All at once, a gust of wind swept down the road, peppering them with gravel and dust. The trees beside the road swayed dangerously, creaking ominously.

"Ow, that hurt," Sam cried, rubbing her eyes.

"Don't rub them, honey, you'll make it worse," he cautioned her, pulling her hands away.

Sam's eyes were red. She squinted at him, the right eye tearing up. Chris could see a couple of specks of dark matter within it.

"Okay, we need to wash your eye out before that gravel scratches your cornea," he stated glumly.

As if things couldn't get worse, the heavens opened, and a sheet of heavy rain pounded against them.

"Daddy," Sam wailed.

He lifted her into his arms and ran towards the squat bungalow, hoping that Seal Islanders were the welcoming type.

He placed Sam on her two feet and pounded on the door but received no response.

He tried the door handle. The house was unlocked. The door swung wide.

"Hello," he called into the house. "I'm sorry to bother you, but my daughter has got something in her eye and it's raining pretty hard."

"Daddy, I don't like this," Sam whimpered, hugging his side.

"Hello, anyone here," he yelled once more.

No one answered.

"Come on, let's get you fixed up," he told her, leading the way into the house.

Chris tugged his daughter through the living room and into the tiny kitchen.

"Here, rinse your eyes out," he ordered her.

Sam ran the water into the sink and did as her father told her, flushing the dirt and dust from both eyes.

"It burns," she sobbed.

"I know it does, baby, but you'll be okay," he replied gently, dabbing the tears from her eyes with a dish towel.

Sam sniffled and pulled herself together.

Chris opened the cupboards. There were cans of soup and some boxes of dried goods, but not a lot. He checked the fridge and found it was empty.

"I don't think anyone lives here," he said, putting two and two together. "Come on, let's check out the rest of the house."

"What if we get caught," Sam whined.

"We'll say we were hired to check on the house," he answered smugly.

Chris wandered through the small rancher, moseying through the two bedrooms. He returned to the living room and found some old mail on a side table. The name on the bills was Tammy Smith.

There were photos of Tammy and her family around the house. Many were faded with age, most black and white. Since there were no pictures of kids or grandchildren, it looked like Tammy Smith was a spinster. Good for the Nicholas family, not so good for Tammy Smith.

The rain battered the windows. It bounced off the back-porch's tin roof.

"I think our friend Tammy must have passed away," Chris announced, returning to the galley-style kitchen where his daughter still huddled. "Let's make some hot soup and hunker down until the storm blows over."

"In a dead lady's house," Sam shivered.

"I don't think she'd mind," Chris hugged his daughter. "Look at that picture. Doesn't she look like a nice old lady to you?"

"No," Sam gasped, staring at the picture of the broad-shouldered woman grimacing into the camera. "She's staring right at me. I don't think she wants us here."

***

Also Russell was happy-happy-happy when Aunt Ida asked

him to walk Pearl Tullis home. He liked Pearl. She liked Also's top hat, and she made the bestest blueberry jam that Also had ever tasted. Maybe she would reward him with blueberry jam on toast.

"I think that was the most entertaining wedding that I've ever been to," Pearl huffed as they emerged onto the flatter section of South Shore Road.

"That was my very first wedding," Also chimed. "Are all weddings funny like that?"

Also's arm ached from holding up the old lady so she wouldn't fall. She was ancient, like Watchtower Mountain and dinosaur bones in museums. Also bet Pearl was as old as Watchtower Mountain, maybe even older, but not as old as dinosaurs. They were super-duper old. His momma told him never to ask a lady her age so he didn't dare ask. Momma said that was rude. Also prided himself on never being rude.

"No, weddings aren't always happy places," Pearl guffawed. "Sometimes families aren't that nice to each other, especially when they get together all in one place."

"That's silly," he frowned, not sure if Pearl was kidding him.

"I agree," Pearl sighed. "And I think brides and grooms from now until eternity should have a pig and a cow present, or at least one of them."

Also grinned. He loved Peaches. The cow's nose was velvety soft. Gertrude terrified him. She was pushy and kept trying to eat his hat.

Pearl let go of his arm once they were past Morris Tweedsmuir's farm. He saw Brutus, one of Aunt Ida's Saint Bernard's, in Morris' yard, but he was tied to a tree so he couldn't visit with Also.

Also smirked. He guessed that Brutus wasn't Aunt Ida's dog anymore since he lived with Morris.

Also waved to the humongous Saint Bernard.

The dog woofed lightly, drool dripping from its mouth, its big eyes fixed on Also.

Also noticed two people in the distance walking down the

road as he and Pearl approached the white picket fence border-
ing Pearl's property. The two people were almost at the laughing
lady's house when a gust of wind blew his top hat off his head
and down the road.

"My hat," Also cried, chasing after the hat as the wind kept
rolling it out of his reach, his coat tails billowing behind him.

"Watch out for that tree branch," Pearl warned as he raced
after the hat skipping along the road.

The hat dodged right and then left, faster than a basketball
player dribbling a ball down the court, until finally it snagged on
a willow bush.

Also stooped to pick it up and almost poked his eye out. Next
time, he'd pay better attention to what Pearl had to say.

Stupid wind, he grunted. He sighed with relief when his finger
closed around the hat's brim and popped it back on his head,
keeping one hand on top of his head to keep it from blowing
away again.

"Come in quick, Also, the storm is upon us," Pearl shouted over
the driving wind. "You can stay with me until it blows over."

The lanky boy ran across the road, still holding onto his hat, a
wide grin on his pudgy face. Now he would get to have a dollop
of the world's number one blueberry jam on toast.

Suddenly, a raindrop pelted him in the face. More and more
raindrops followed it.

Also glanced down the road in time to see the little girl
and her father dash through the gate of Aunt Ida and Pearl's
friend's house. Also called Tammy Smith 'The Laughing Lady'
because when he played a joke on her, she fell down laughing.
She laughed so hard that she couldn't get up. He wondered if he
should tell Pearl about the two people when the rain began to fall
heavier and heavier.

"Pearl, the rain is making my hat sick," he screamed, horrified
as his hat burst at the seams.

"Get inside, Also," Pearl waved to him, holding the front door
open.

Also raced past her into the house, tears streaming down his face, all thoughts of the man and little girl flying from his mind. His hat folded in on itself. Russell 'Also' Russell began wailing in earnest.

Pugs & Pernicious Parrots

December 12th - early afternoon

It wasn't often that Sam wasn't happy, but today was a doozie of a down-and-outer. When the neighbors came over and asked what they were doing in the house, her dad had turned on the charm.

"Tammy was a good friend of my lawyer's mother," he said, fixing the couple next door with a high beamed thousand-watt-light-up-the-sky smile. "He's looking after the Estate. He asked us to stay for a few days to do some clean up around the place."

Daddy was so sincere that Sam almost bought the lie.

"Oh, that's marvelous. She was a lovely lady," the forty something bleached blond crooned. "We miss her."

"I don't," the woman's husband mumbled.

"How'd she die," Sam queried, her father casting a warning glance her way.

"Heart attack," the man commented dryly. "Some fool boy pulled a prank on her."

"Well, at least she died laughing," the wife snorted in amusement.

Sam and Chris were taken aback – 'died laughing'. Was the woman serious? Chris glanced down at his daughter and shrugged.

Sam frowned. She didn't want to stay in a house where an old woman died, laughing or not. It was creepy.

"Anyway, we've closed our cottage for the winter and are heading back to Vancouver," the woman continued, her husband rolling his eyes at the obvious. They were both standing in the road with suitcases in hand.

"We'll keep an eye on your place while we're here," Chris grinned.

Her father would keep an eye on their cottage all right, Sam thought. The couple had just handed him an invitation to help himself to whatever he wanted.

The two neighbors bid them farewell and walked down the road, pulling their suitcases behind them. The road was uneven, so it made for quite a comical sight. The cases kept getting stuck in a rut or falling over. Either this couple wasn't very well liked or no one on the island owned a car.

"Listen, I'm going to fetch some groceries off the catamaran for you. I want you to stay here while I go do a few more jobs," Chris told her, steering Sam back into the house.

"Noooo," Sam wailed. "You aren't going without me."

"Sweetie, I'll be back before you know it," he consoled her. "There must be a hundred videos in the living room. I bet you haven't seen half of those movies... and there are books too."

Sam pouted. Tears welled in her eyes.

She didn't want to stay in a dead woman's house.

"What if something happens to you," she sniffed. "What if you get hurt and need help and I'm not there?"

The 'what ifs' neared panic levels.

What if a ghost got her?

What if she had a bad dream?

What if she cut a finger opening a can of soup?

What if she just plain got scared?

"I'll be fine," Chris knelt beside his daughter and wrapped her in a hug. "I'll be back in two days at the latest. You're a big girl now. You can do it."

"Fine," she grumbled, wrapping her arms around his shoulders, "but if you aren't back in two days, I'm calling the police."

The two of them laughed together.

Sam didn't feel like laughing, but she didn't want her daddy worrying about her. He might make a mistake. That would be bad... really bad.

Sam would never call the police. She wasn't a snitch. She

didn't like it, though. Daddy had left her alone on the boat before, but only for one night. Two nights was pushing it. She was only nine.

Sam opened a can of Campbell's tomato soup. She added some Carnation milk and water and put it on the stove to boil. Daddy had only been gone for two hours and it felt like forever. At least she hadn't cut a finger opening the can though.

She looked out the kitchen window and saw a chubby red-faced boy wearing a pointy tailed black over a blue sweater and a thing on his head that looked like a lump of coal. A gigantic grey and white pig and a cream-colored cow with the biggest eyes Sam had ever seen stood beside him. They stared through the kitchen window at her.

Sam shrieked.

***

Benny Lee and his crew sauntered across the dock and landing, heading towards the Bristling Boar pub, a grey parrot balanced precariously on his shoulder.

"What shall we do with the drunken sailor," the parrot sang. "What shall we do with the drunken sailor?"

"Ugh, not that one again," Benny's first mate groaned.

"At least he ain't swearing," the second crewman grinned.

"Yet," Benny chuckled.

"Phoenix is really gonna take him," the first mate asked, his brows furrowing together in puzzlement.

"Lift up her skirts and do her matey," the parrot sang in tune to the old sea shanty.

"Yep. He said to leave him at the pub," Benny replied, casting a furtive glance toward the parrot on his shoulder. The bird cocked his head sideways and lifted a foot and flicked it up and down.

Was that bird waving goodbye to him?

Darned bird was evil, Benny glowered, guilt nibbling at his guts. Reggie hadn't wanted it at all, but Benny couldn't stand it any longer. He had thought it would be fun owing a parrot. What a big mistake that was. No wonder the pet shop owner had sold him cheap.

"Hey, baby-baby," the bird chirped, rolling its eyes at the first mate. "Buh-buh-buh-baby."

"We'll be banned from the pub for life," the crewman stammered, yanking open the door to the Bristling Boar.

The pub was hopping. Benny wondered why until he realized folks were still partying a day after the wedding. It must have been a real shindig.

"Oy, no pets in the pub," Stew yelled from behind the bar.

"He's not a pet, he's a bird," Benny winked at the pub owner. "Besides, you let the pig in."

"I don't care what he is, get him out of here," Stew growled, wagging a beefy finger at Benny. "And I don't let Gertrude in, she lets herself in."

"Put him in the scuppers with a hose pipe on him," the parrot sang. "Penny for a pint. Penny for a pint."

The pub patrons cheered.

"I'd pay a penny for a pint, Stew," one old man jeered.

"And I wouldn't mind seeing ya tossed in the scuppers," a bleary-eyed fisherman yelled back.

"Aye, the parrot's buying," another joked.

Benny grinned. The African grey was a hit.

"Reggie told me to leave Mac with you," Benny said, sinking into the last barstool. His two crewmen drifted away into the crowd. Cowards, Benny thought.

"And where am I gonna put a bird like that," Stew thundered, pouring Benny a draft.

Mac the Black of the Caribbean, the parrot's original name, swiveled his head around so that he was looking at Stew upside down. He then let out a raspberry. Benny thought the pub owner would wring its neck, but the aging bartender burst out laughing.

"I dunno where your gonna put him," Benny confessed. "He's my wedding present to Reg. Reg just said to drop him off here. His name is Mac the Black of the Caribbean, but I just call him

Mac."

"Ain't this parrot from Africa," Stew queried, puzzled.

"He is," Benny responded. "I didn't name him."

Stew pulled out a bag of peanuts from under the bar and poured some into a wooden bowl. The parrot eyed him with interest. Stew grinned and put the peanut bowl on the bar.

The parrot walked down Benny's arm and onto the slippery bar. Mac cooed as he fell on his face.

Benny moaned inwardly.

Please don't screw this up, Mac.

"And it's no-nay-never right up your kilt," the parrot's voice warbled, slip sliding towards the bowl of peanuts.

Stew slapped his leg and roared with laughter.

"I like this bird," he beamed. "I can see why Reggie wants him. Betty won't be impressed, but if Reg wants us to look after him until the honeymooners get back, well then, we will."

Stew grabbed a dry wash towel from the sink and put it on the bar for the parrot to walk on. The parrot strolled across the towel like it was going for a walk in the park and then dived into the peanut bowl. Peanut husks flew in every direction.

"We're gonna have to work on your manners, Mac," Stew chortled and wandered back down the bar to fill a few more drink orders.

Benny felt the weight of the world sluff off his shoulders. By the time Reggie returned, he'd be long gone.

Benny smiled and shouted out an order for a burger and fries. He'd have to watch the time. He didn't want to be here when the parrot finished the peanuts.

***

Reggie guided *The Persephone* along the coastline. A thin layer of mist floated over the water. The clouds hung low over the inland mountains.

His hands gripped the wheel, the knuckles knobby with arthritis. His knees were stiffening up too. The weather was changing; his bones were telling him so.

Reggie took a sip of coffee and cast an uneasy glance skyward. The clouds were roiling like foam in an expresso.

A squat church stood on the point wrapped in fog. Icy tendrils billowed around the gravestones between the church and the clifftop like voracious wraiths searching for lost souls.

The church and office buildings were all shut up tight.

There was a band of yellow police tape strung atop the cliff, some of it still taut, while other sections had collapsed to the ground.

Reggie shivered. Bad things had happened in that place. Murder. Theft. Deceit. Bodies cut into pieces. Graves desecrated.

He pushed the throttle forward and the old boat sliced through the water, putting some distance between the trawler and the haunted church and graveyard.

Welcome to Lund, he thought, as the quaint seaside town came into view a few minutes later. It was a lovely spot, normally one of his favorite places.

Today, the marina was empty. The pub would be on reduced hours, the peak tourist season long since over. He considered stopping in and then decided against it, not wanting folks to hassle Betty for her part in making the town famous for all the wrong reasons.

Betty was below decks reading a book, the German shepherd curled up on the bed beside her.

The thought of his wife in his bed, reading glasses perched on her nose, the dog's head resting in her lap, snuggled cozily beneath a quilt, lost in a fictional world made him smile. The image made him blush too; his thoughts turning carnal.

The Persephone's bow cut into the light surf with precision, the waves minor ripples on the grey-black waters of the strait.

He started, spotting a huge deadhead in the water, and turned hard to starboard to avoid it. The log was wide and at least twenty feet long. A salvager had flagged it. The trawler's hull glanced lightly off one end. The half-submerged log would have shattered the trawler's hull like a battering ram if he'd hit it any harder.

Reggie shook his head and focused on steering the boat. Thoughts of a honeymoon romp had to wait a little while.

Reggie decided Stuart Island was the best place to anchor for lunch. He wanted to stop at Alert Bay for the night and introduce Betty to some of his old friends. In all their travels, they hadn't had a chance to do that yet. He planned on taking her to explore the Broughton Archipelago Conservancy the next day. It was a magnificent spot, wild and untouched.

The day-old stubble on his cheek bristled as he scratched his chin. His eyes drooped, the long day yesterday and the even longer night making him weary. He chuckled at the thought of last night. All his dreams had been fulfilled and then some.

Stop that, he scolded himself. *Where there is one deadhead, there may be more.*

He opened the window and inhaled the crisp scent of the salt water. The north wind ruffled his hair, the cold biting into his face. The tiredness sloughed off him.

Powell River and Lund now far behind him, the dark green crescent of Stuart Island appeared out of the mist. A smattering of hail hit the windshield.

"Hey, Bets," he called over his shoulder.

"Yes, hon," his wife answered from down below.

His wife... he prayed he would never get over the heat that those two words drew from inside his breast... *his wife.*

"Stuart Island's coming up. Thought we could have some of that there smoked salmon we got in the cupboard and some soup. It's starting to hail. Feels like a soup kind of day," he said.

"Okay," Betty agreed. "I'll pull it out and start making some sandwiches. You want mayo or cream cheese on your sandwich?"

"Both."

Reggie smiled. Life was good, even if the weather wasn't.

"Want some wine with that," she asked, poking her head out of the hatch. "I think I can squeeze two glasses of Chablis out of the bottle we opened last night."

"Fine by me," he grinned. "Turn the heater up too, a nor-easter is coming in. It's cold as a witch's tit on deck."

Ice pellets bounced off the deck and windshield. Reggie was about to close the window when he saw a small speck of brown race across the pebbly beach along the waterfront of the bay that he was aiming for.

The Persephone's engines rumbled as he throttled the big diesel down and drifted into the half-moon shaped inlet.

The grey-haired sea captain squinted into the rolling fog.

There it was again.

A little bundle of golden brown darted back and forth across the beach.

It was too big to be a rabbit and too small to be a wolf, plus there weren't any wolves on Stuart Island. At least, not that he knew of. It could be a fox, but he didn't think there were any foxes on the island either. It definitely wasn't a racoon; it was the wrong color.

Reggie picked up the binoculars he kept in the wheelhouse and looked through them.

"Bets, put a hold on those sandwiches," he yelled to his wife.

"Why?" she hollered back.

"Because we got us a rescue mission," Reggie drawled, stopping the engine and letting the trawler drift in as close to shore as he was willing to go.

"What are we rescuing," Betty asked, emerging from the cabin, the shepherd padding along behind her.

"A dog," he scowled, handing Betty the binoculars.

Betty smirked, thinking her husband was joking, until she lifted the binoculars and looked through them.

"It's a pug," she gasped. "What on earth is a pug doing out here?"

"Probably fell off a boat," Reggie replied with a shake of his head. It happened every year, boaters losing their dogs overboard, hikers hiking the West Coast Trail losing their dogs to the wilderness. Sometimes there were happy endings, but most times the dogs died out here, city dogs unable to survive in the wilds. The West Coast could be a dangerous place.

"Poor thing is a bone wrack," she fumed, handing Reggie the binoculars.

"I'll drop anchor and we'll go fetch him," Reggie said, springing into action. "Bring some of that salmon to coax him to us. Gawd only knows what the wee thing has been through."

Betty nodded and ducked back through the hatch to the galley.

Outside the warm cabin, the hail turned into rain.

Small mercies, the old fisherman thought, as he tugged on his rain slicker.

"You may as well come, Champ," he told the German shepherd. "Just don't scare him away. You gotta think small, like that wee mutt."

The dog whined and wagged his tail.

Reggie gave him a pat and set about dropping the anchor and readying the dinghy.

He thanked the gods of old that the sea was calm despite the sheets of rain that pounded against the trawler and the rocky beach. He knew the weather could turn far worse at any moment and prayed that the little dog would come to them right away.

Raspberry Beret

December 12th – late afternoon

The young man outside the window waved vigorously, a wide grin on his face. To his left, the doe-eyed cow nibbled off the tops of the few flowers that struggled to survive. The pig stood still, snout in the air, nostrils quivering.

Sam stopped screaming.

The odd threesome looked harmless enough, and Daddy never said she couldn't make new friends.

She put the pot of tomato soup aside, turned off the stove, and headed for the door.

"Hello," she offered, opening the front door wide.

"Hello," the boy mimicked her.

Even Sam knew that there was something special about the boy, his earnest round face, and sparkling slightly Asian looking eyes.

"I'm making soup," Sam said, looking quizzically from the animals to the boy.

"What kind of soup," he asked innocently.

"Tomato," she replied. "Would you like some?"

"Yes, please," he grinned, removing the thing from the top of his head and bowing with a flourish of the black rag in his hand. Sam read about that in a book once, gentlemen bowing to ladies. It was quite marvelous.

"My name is Samantha, but Daddy calls me Sam," she said, stepping aside.

"I'm Russell Russell, but everyone calls me Also," he laughed, opening the garden gate, and striding into the yard.

Gertrude barged in after him, followed by Peaches.

"No, Gertie, stay out," Also yelled, trying to push the pig back out of the gate. "You too, Peaches. You can't come in here."

Also's lower lip quivered as he ran back and forth between the pig and cow, his hands flapping wildly. Neither animal seemed concerned.

"It's okay," Sam laughed. "I'm supposed to clean up the yard, but they can do it for me."

Also stopped flailing and sighed wearily.

"They never listen to me," he huffed.

"What's their names," Sam asked, tentatively stepping out onto the porch.

"This is Gertrude," Also replied, wrapping an arm around the errant pig now snout deep in Tammy's vegetable garden. The pot-bellied pig pulled up a rotting turnip and grunted in pleasure. "I call her Gertie. The cow is Peaches. She's a peach."

Sam giggled.

"Is she friendly?"

"Oh, yes, Sam, my new friend," Also grinned.

Sam cautiously approached the pot-bellied pig. The pig dwarfed the little girl. Gertrude turned her snot and turnip covered snout towards Sam.

"Ooooh, I don't want cooties, Gertrude," Sam yelped, pulling back.

Also roared with laughter.

"You gotta not be afraid of getting cooties from Gertie," Also beamed. "She's always got cooties."

Sam stood ramrod straight as the pot-bellied pig sniffed her, and then seemingly satisfied the girl was okay, went back to digging up the garden.

Sam let out the breath she was holding and walked over to pat the cow. Peaches continued to nibble the tops off the last of the fall flowers as Sam stroked her neck.

"I like Peaches," Sam cooed.

"Me too," Also said, "but I like soup too."

Sam giggled. Also was funny.

"Come on, let's get some soup then," the raven-haired girl

offered, and then impulsively kissed the cow on the forehead.

Also clapped his hands together in glee.

"Want to go digging for treasure after soup," Also asked. "That was where I was going when I stopped and saw you in the laughing lady's kitchen."

A pang of fear rippled through her breast.

Was this the boy that pulled the joke on the lady who lived here? It must have been a doozer of a joke.

Maybe Sam shouldn't let him in? Not if his jokes killed people.

Sam looked deep into the sublime face of her new friend, at the lump of material glued to his head, the hat that used to be a hat, and then at his two four-legged friends. The pig and cow seemed happy with his company. Shen then asked a very grown up question: "One shovel or two?"

"Hmmm, maybe just one to start," the young man replied thoughtfully. "I'm bigger than you so I can probably dig longer and maybe you can help Also decide where to dig."

"Works for me," Sam quipped. "Let's eat. I'm sure there's a shovel around here someplace."

Russell 'Also' Russell cheered and tore the lump of felt off his head and threw it into the air. It landed at Gertrude's feet. The pig quickly ate it.

Also wailed in horror.

Sam rushed to his side and pulled the petrified boy into the house lest people come running and wonder what a little girl was doing in a dead lady's house all by herself.

"Come on, Also, let's find you a new hat," she said, slamming the door shut behind them. "I bet the lady who lived here wouldn't mind you having one of her hats at all."

"Really," Also sniffled.

"After the soup, we'll find you a new hat, and then go treasure hunting."

Also clapped his hands together once again.

"Sam, my new friend, you're the best friend ever," he beamed.

Sam's heart soared. She had never had a friend before. Maybe it wasn't such a bad thing that Daddy had gone away for a couple of days. Daddy might not like Also.

***

Reggie rowed the dinghy to shore, the rain pelting down upon his head and shoulders. Betty huddled in the boat's prow, one arm around the soaking wet German shepherd. Champ sat with his ears pinned against his head, his tail tucked beneath him, eyes squinting in the driving rain. The little dinghy was quickly filling up with water.

The aluminum hull scraped against rock. Reggie pulled up the oars and tucked them beneath the bench seats for safety.

The clouds were now so low and the rain so heavy that he could barely make out the lines of the black hulled and red trimmed trawler moored in the bay.

"Okay, Champ, go find him," Betty ordered the shepherd.

The dog jumped into the surf and raced off across the rocky beach, nose to the ground.

Reggie doubted there would be much to smell.

The old fisherman followed the dog into the light surf and offered Betty his hand. She grabbed it and gingerly stepped out of the boat, trying not to slip on the slick rocks below the surface.

"He's probably in the trees somewhere," she remarked, pushing a wet hair out of her face. Mist dotted her pale eyelashes and the tiny hairs on her face.

"Yar, Mother Nature must'a been holding this one in fer a long time," the seaman mumbled.

Betty chuckled as she sloshed her way into shore, her black gumboots and yellow rubber rain pants squeaking as she walked.

Reggie pulled the dinghy high above the tide line.

"We needs ta find him lickety-split," he grumbled. "It's only a matter of time afore the winds pick up."

"Yeah, I feel it too," Betty replied worriedly.

They heard Champ barking in the distance.

"Good dog," Betty beamed, scurrying across the rocky beach,

hands tucked inside the slicker's pockets.

Water dripped off Reggie's hood and onto his face as he studied the gnarled cedars and firs in the forest. The foliage was dark green and healthy looking, the trunks covered in thick moss. Many of the trees were twisted sideways from being battered year-round by the prevailing winds.

It was a miracle the little dog had survived.

Champ stood at the edge of the forest, whimpering, his tail wagging furiously. He glanced nervously over at Betty and Reggie as they approached.

Beneath a salal bush, something squirmed, sending water cascading down from the struggling evergreen that grew out of the barren ground.

Betty squatted beside the shepherd and pulled a piece of smoked salmon out of her pocket.

"Come on pup, let's get you someplace warm," she crooned to the frightened pug.

The pug poked its silver and black nose out of the bush. It barked. The bark was shrill and filled with heartbreak. The wee dog's eyes were weepy.

"Ah, yer poor tyke," Reggie stammered, kneeling beside Betty.

Champ whined and licked Betty's face as she held the salmon out farther.

The pug darted out of the bush and snapped the salmon out of her fingers, its tail windmilling in happy circles. Betty scooped the frail old dog up, tears welling in her eyes.

"Give him here for a minute," Reggie's baritone voice rumbled. "Open yer coat and hold him against yer sweater. Poor nub is shivering up a storm."

"He's so thin," Betty cried, handing the pug to her husband.

Champ licked his lips and raced off. He had completed one duty, but there were others to finish.

Reggie watched the German shepherd romp, his tail wagging despite the weather. The pug trembled in his hands and licked his face.

"Yer a real trooper, aren't ya," he whispered to the frail pup.

Betty zipped open her slicker and took the dog back. She tucked the pug inside her coat and zipped the slicker back up, cradling it against her breast. The dog let out a long sigh of relief.

The wind brushed the hair out of her face, signaling that the major storm that Reggie had feared was upon them.

"Come on," he hissed. "We gotta git while the getting's good."

"I hear you, Mister Phoenix," his wife purred.

Reggie grinned as they stamped across the beach to the dinghy. They didn't need to call Champ. He was already sitting in the rowboat, his business done.

Reggie pushed the boat into the water. Betty climbed in, her husband holding her under her arm to keep her from falling. The pug was a little lump under Betty's yellow rain slicker.

The seaman rowed for all he was worth as the whitecaps grew taller, the north-easter that he had been worrying about hitting the coast full force within minutes.

He struggled to get the dinghy lined up with the boat so that Champ and Betty could get out safely. Champ bravely leapt onto the dive platform fastened to the trawler's stern. Betty followed the shepherd.

"I'll put the dogs in the wheelhouse and come back and help," Betty yelled over the rising storm.

Reggie nodded. He held tight to the pitching trawler, the dinghy bucking like a bronco. He tried to tie a line around the iron mooring hook on the dive platform, but was foiled at every attempt.

Betty raced to the wheelhouse, Champ scurrying across the deck behind her, his paws slithering across the waterlogged surface.

An enormous wave caught the skiff and heaved it upwards. Reggie toppled forwards. He lost an oar. A giant wave hit the trawler. Surf funneled up between the dinghy and the trawler like a geyser.

The little boat sailed upwards.

A gust of wind caught it.

The dinghy rolled over, throwing Reggie into the roiling

water.

"Reggggiieeee," he heard Betty scream as the dinghy's gunwale hit him in the head.

Salt water cascaded down inside his slicker and boots, dragging him beneath the surface. Reggie flailed, desperately trying to kick off his gumboots.

The icy water knocked his breath away.

A kettle drum banged inside his head.

He sank farther and farther beneath the waves. He could just barely see the hull of *The Persephone* above him as he drifted away from it.

He kicked and kicked, refusing to give up.

Finally, one boot slipped off and then the other. He became more buoyant, rising a few inches towards the surface. His fingers were numb. He could barely hold onto his coat's zipper as he fought to undo it. Every joint and muscle in his body screamed from the cold.

He cursed himself for his stubbornness, refusing to wear one of the old red lifejackets he kept in the hold. He had given Betty the only inflatable life vest he had. Old habits die hard.

He swallowed a mouthful of seawater. It was bitter with remorse. Dying beneath the waves one day into his honeymoon was too much to bear. Gawd, he was a fool.

He kicked one last time. It was all he had left.

Let go, Davy, let go, he prayed.

The zipper on his coat gave way.

He shot to the surface.

There... within grasp... was a round orange ring. He grabbed hold of it as he gulped in precious air.

"Hold on," his wife hollered over the storm.

He smiled as the beautiful, unflappable woman he married hauled him in like a two-hundred-pound tuna.

"I love you," he stuttered, his hands wrapping around the rigging at the back of the trawler, his wife reaching for him, her grey eyes filled with determination.

***

"Did you know it's only thirteen days until Christmas," Also sang, dancing down the road like Snoopy, nose in the air, a red raspberry beret smelling of mothballs on his head, coattails flying. He used the long-handled shovel like a cane and kicked up his heels, spinning in the air.

Sam danced the Snoopy-dance beside him, twirling like a ballerina, laughing and hooting with glee.

"I didn't," she rejoiced.

"I already wrote him a letter and asked him for a magic trick kit," Also giggled. "I want to be a magician."

"How about I ask Santa for you," Sam's voice warbled.

She bit her lip and stopped spinning, catching herself at the last minute.

Oh, oh, she shouldn't have said that. Daddy will be mad.

"You know Santa," Also squawked.

Sam didn't think Also's brown eyes could go any rounder, but they did.

"I just meant that in my letter to Santa I can ask him to get you a magic trick kit too," she stammered.

"Wow, you're my bestest friend," Also beamed.

Sam giggled. Also was her bestest friend too, but she better be more careful.

Gertrude waddled along behind them like she wore an imaginary leash. Peaches had decided to stay at Tammy Smith's and continue grazing her way through the garden.

"Does Gertie always follow you around like that," Sam asked, walking backwards.

"Gertie does what Gertie does," Also shrugged, spinning around to walk backwards like Sam.

"Huh," Sam snorted, not quite sure what that meant.

She was still a little fearful of the pig, but Gertrude was cute in an ugly-duckling sort of way.

"Gertie's a hero, did you know that?" the boy asked her.

"She is?"

"Yep, she helped solve the severed feet case," Also replied earnestly. "Gertie's momma is Betty Bruce. She's a detective. No wait, Betty Bruce is Betty Phoenix cuz she just got married. I know that cuz I was there."

Sam gasped.

The pig belongs to a copper.

"Gertie also found the Brother's treasure. That's where we're going now," Also cheered, lifting the shovel to the sky. "We're going to Brother Twelve's cabin. That's where Gertie found it."

"I think I know where that is," Sam mumbled, her mind a jumble of thoughts. "There're holes everywhere around it."

"Yep," Also nodded as they reached the end of the road.

The forest trail zigzalled through the bushes in front of them.

"The cabin has a grass roof and its really old," Sam said, not sure if she should go any farther. She wanted to go on a treasure hunt but wondered if it wasn't a really bad idea. Hanging out with a pig belonging to a copper would send her father off the deep end.

"What's the matter," Also asked, sensing her disquiet.

"I'm not sure I should go there without my daddy's permission and he's at work," she replied.

Also smirked, stubbing a sneakered toe against the ground. Gertrude caught up to them, nosed Also and then turned towards Sam.

Sam could have sworn that the pig knew exactly what she was thinking.

The pot bellied pig scented the air, squealed, and raced up the trail, her curly tail spinning furiously.

"Gertie, come back," Also shouted and raced after the pig, using the shovel to part the shrubs that crowded the trail.

"Also, wait," Sam hollered, running after her friend.

***

Morris Tweedsmuir swept the metal detector back and forth over the hole where Gertrude had unearthed the prophet's treasure while his Saint Bernard, Brutus, dug deeper into the sides of another hole several feet away.

"Nothing," he grumbled.

Dirt flew everywhere as the giant fluffy white and brown dog tunneled under the roots of a tree.

Morris ignored him and stepped down into the bottom of the well where the box of gold coins had been buried. If there was one, there had to be more.

He couldn't believe it when Betty and Reggie had turned most of the gold over to the government and donated the rest to charity. He certainly wouldn't have done that. If anything, he'd keep his mouth shut, maybe rebury it in his backyard and take just as much out at a time as he needed.

"I wouldn't have to work another day in my life," he told the dog.

The dog looked up and woofed.

Thundering hooves and the crash of brush heralded Gertrude's arrival.

"Now you git home, Gertie," Morris chastised the pig. "This is my dig now."

Brutus barked happily and greeted the pig.

"Holy cow, that dog's bigger than the pig," a little girl cried breathlessly.

Morris spun around in time to see that crazy boy, Also Russell, and a raven-haired girl that he didn't recognize, looking down at him. The girl's eyes were icy blue. The intelligent, knowing gaze she fixed upon him unnerved the goat farmer.

"Who the heck are ya," the red-haired man sputtered.

"Yeah, well who the heck are you and what're you doing in that hole," the girl countered.

The kid was a tiny thing, but the defiance in her stare and aura of authority set Morris to worrying. He didn't want anyone knowing he was still out looking for treasure.

The Saint Bernard galloped after the pig as Gertrude made a beeline for the shore.

"Brutus," he hollered after the dog.

The dog came bounding back and jumped into the hole,

knocking the metal detector out of his hand.

"What's that stick you got there, Morris," Also asked. "It don't look like my shovel."

"It's a metal detector," Sam replied. "He's searching for treasure too."

Also's lower lip sagged with disappointment.

"No, I'm not," Morris stuttered. "I'm just making sure Betty got everything, is all."

"Yeah, right," the girl grinned.

"Yeah, well ya haven't answered my question," he scolded her. "Who are ya? You ain't from around here."

"Nope, I'm not," the girl countered.

"This is my friend, Sam," Also replied for her.

Sam elbowed the odd boy.

They were an odd pair, the frizzy bearded man standing in the hole thought, a pale-faced snippet of a girl and a tall teen wearing a red beret.

"What are ya doing out with Also," Morris asked suspiciously, pushing the dog away and climbing out of the hole. "And where are yer folks?"

"That's none of your business," the lippy child replied.

"It's okay, Sam, Morris is my friend too," Also answered, his face the picture of innocence.

"He's not my friend, Also, and my daddy said I'm not to talk to strangers," she whispered to the boy.

Also nodded in understanding.

Just then, Peaches came crashing through the brush at a jog, looking for Gertrude.

"She's gone that-away, Peaches," Also informed the cow, pointing to the beach.

"They're off to see Rainbow, I expect," Morris twittered.

"Come on, Also, we'll come back again," Sam grinned evilly. "There's one too many treasure hunters here for my liking."

"Oh, okay," Also sobbed, crestfallen.

Morris sighed. The boy was a good kid. Special is what they called folks like him now.

"That a new hat," Morris remarked, nodding towards the raspberry colored beret.

"Sam my friend gave it to me," the teen chimed happily.

The girl kissed Morris's dog on the top of the head. Brutus seemed infatuated by her. Morris guessed she couldn't be all bad, but personally, he wouldn't let his kid wander alone in the bushes with a teenaged boy, no matter how nice the boy was.

He'd have to keep an eye on her.

"Off ya go and ya be careful around here," he warned them. "The Brother, he don't like kids."

"You mean you've seen his ghost," Also cried fearfully.

"I means exactly that," Morris nodded agreement.

The Saint Bernard jumped back into the hole he had been playing in and started digging once more. The girl watched the dog dig for some time before turning to look Morris square in the eye.

"There's no such thing as ghosts," she glowered. "My daddy told me that."

"I suppose ya don't believe in Santa either," he snapped back.

"Oh, I know there's a Santa," she grinned cheekily and scampered off, dragging the boy in the topcoat with her.

All at once, the wind started to howl through the trees and a smattering of rain hit the ground.

"Come on, Brutus, time to go," the angry man growled at the dog.

Old Dogs and Baubles

December 12th – night

Betty found herself mesmerized by the soft drizzle pitter-pattering against the roof of the wheelhouse and the gentle slosh of water bouncing off the hull of *The Persephone* as she sat in a chair, the white muzzled pug wrapped in a warm blanket on her lap. Mugsy snored lightly, content to have a full belly and a human being to hold it. Betty had come up with the name. It seemed fitting.

Lord only knew what the old dog had been through. That it had survived more than a few days on the island was a miracle. Given how thin it was, the dog had been there for a while.

The storm that raged all afternoon had finally died down. Rivulets of rainwater streamed down the windshield and gathered in small pools on the deck. The red and white lights along the deck glistened under the blackening sky. Stuart Island was an obsidian blot within the deeper darkness of the cloudy night.

"I'm glad we hunkered down here fer the night," Reggie said.

"Me too," she replied. "It is so peaceful."

"Yeah, ya don't get many folks up this way at this time of year," he agreed.

"That's what's been puzzling me," Betty continued, her face taking on a pensive look.

"Oh?"

"How did Mugsy end up on that island? It's off the beaten path and the tourists are long gone," Betty remarked, her voice hardening as she met her husband's gaze.

"I know," he said, letting out a long breath. "I can't imagine anyone dumping an old dog on a remote island to die."

As if on cue, the radio crackled into life.

"*Persephone*, Alert Bay. Over," a man's deep voice blared over the radio.

"Alert Bay, *Persephone*. Over," Reggie responded, adjusting the radio's volume.

"I made some inquires for you, Reg," the man said. "Seems like nobody reported a missing pug. We've got a Border collie and a grey and white Pitbull that still haven't been found. One went missing on the West Coast Trail a month or two ago and the other fell off a boat in Desolation Sound. No little dogs though."

"Aye well thanks fer checking fer us," Reggie growled. "If'n ya hear anything then give 'em my cell number. I don't think anyone's gonna pry this mug out of my wife's arms any time soon."

The radio crackled twice.

Betty grinned. She expected the radio operator in Alert Bay was having a good laugh.

"Safe travels, *Persephone*. Over," came the man's strangled reply. "See you tomorrow."

Yep, he had been laughing all right.

"Will do. *Persephone*, out. Over," Reggie responded.

"Well, Mugsy, welcome to the clan," Betty whispered to the sleeping pug. The pup opened one rheumy eye, snorted, and then went back to sleep.

"Let's hope Gertie and Peaches don't trample him," Reggie mumbled. "Champ seems to have taken a liking to the little guy."

Champ whined and stood up. He snuffled the pug just to make sure the old dog was still alive and then laid back down, his head on Betty's feet.

"I won't be letting Mugsy near Gert or Peaches for a while," Betty agreed. "He can stay right where he's happiest, in my arms."

"Me too," Reggie joked.

"Awww," Betty beamed. She moved the pug over to one arm and leaned forward to kiss her husband's freshly shaven cheek.

Reggie's satellite phone buzzed. The screen read: Bristling

Boar.

"Stew, what's up, buddy," Reggie said, answering the call.

"When're ya coming to pick up this danged parrot," Stew's voice boomed in reply.

Reggie glanced sideways at Betty.

Parrot?

Betty shrugged.

"What parrot," Reggie asked, confused.

"Your wedding gift from Benny," Stew fumed. "Damnable thing has the foulest mouth I've ever heard. I got people threatening to sue. The crazy bird has already caused three fistfights with guys thinking their mate was hitting on their wife, when it was the bird all along."

Betty smothered a laugh.

"That sneaky fella," Reggie whispered to Betty, his hand over the receiver. "Remember I told ya that Benny wanted to give us a parrot, and I said 'no'. "

"You think he dropped it off at the pub on purpose," Betty mumbled back.

Reggie nodded agreement.

"Well, I'm sorry, Stew, but we weren't expecting any bird, in fact I told Benny we didn't want no parrot," Reggie explained, leaning back in his seat. "I think Benny pulled one over on ya."

"That...," Stew swore.

Reggie turned the sound down on the phone, so he and Betty didn't have to listen to the pub owner rant.

Betty guffawed, startling the two dogs. She quickly covered her mouth with one hand.

"I'm sorry, Stew," Reggie chortled, turning the volume back up, and interrupting the pub owner's tirade, "but the bird's yer problem. We won't be back until just before Christmas and we ain't taking no parrot home."

Reggie held the phone away from his ear as Stew continued to holler. The old fisherman thought he heard the parrot whistle in the background followed by a plea of "show me your thirty-eights and I'll show you my forty-fives".

"See ya in a couple of weeks, buddy," Reggie told his friend, hanging up before the pub owner could comment.

"So, the parrot that your friend wanted to give US for a WEDDING PRESENT has a pottie mouth," Betty quipped, wiping the tears from her eyes.

"Would seem so," Reggie stuttered.

The two of them looked at each other and then wailed with laughter.

***

Sam searched the junk drawers in the kitchen. She pulled out balls of strings, a broken wine bottle opener, umpteen sets of pliers and a bunch of screwdrivers wrapped together in an elastic band.

"Eureka," she yelled, finding what she was looking for.

She pulled a long handled yellow flashlight out of the drawer. She tapped it a couple of times and flicked the black button on the side. The flashlight's beam flashed across the dirty window and back into her eyes.

"Oouch," she squinted, turning the flashlight off.

Sam looked out the window. After the spots in front of her vision faded away, she could see that it was still raining outside, but not as hard as it had earlier. It was the perfect night for earning a living, that's what her father would say.

Dirty dishes and pots filled the sink. She'd get to them later. Right now, she was going on an expedition.

It might not be such a bright idea, given that she was only a kid, but she wanted to investigate the flash of yellow she had seen glittering in the hole that the Saint Bernard had been working at. No one else had seen it, not Also or that crazy bearded guy that didn't like her very much. She had seen it in his eyes. Daddy called guys who lied 'players'. That Morris guy was a player. Also might like him, but she knew a con artist when she saw one. Yep, Morris wasn't no friend of hers.

Sam glanced at the clock on the wall. It was ten o'clock. Daddy would either be casing a job or working on one right now. She was about to go out on her first solo job.

Daddy will be so proud of me, she grinned. *A chip off the old block, that's what he'd call her.*

Sam tugged on an old beige colored raincoat that she found in a closet and a cream-colored wide-brimmed hat. She pulled the hat low over her head to hide her face. It wasn't hard because the hat was way too big for her. The coat went almost to the floor.

Sam grabbed the flashlight off the kitchen table and sneaked out the back door. A short-handled rusty bladed garden shovel stood against the fence. She picked it up and strode out into the night.

It was easy to see the road at first because the five cottages she passed had outside porch lights on. After that, it got blacker than black.

At the end of the road, Sam switched on the flashlight, casting the narrow beam over the trail, her heart beating as fast as a hummingbird's wings.

The forest was wickedly dark. Rain droplets made spattering sounds as they hit the evergreen bushes at the side of the trail.

Also had told her there were no bears or cougars on the island, only wild sheep and a few goats. He said that if you left them be, they'd leave you alone.

Sam gnawed on her lower lip.

"Come on, Sam, you can do it," she stammered, steeling herself to put one foot in front of the other.

She heard a loud rustling in the forest.

"It's only a sheep," she whispered, her heart beating even faster yet.

The rustling grew louder.

A series of loud grunts and squeals followed it.

All at once, her flashlight beam reflected off two beady eyes staring at her out of the darkness.

"Gertrude," she gasped with relief. "You scared me half to death, silly pig."

The pot-bellied pig waddled over to her and stuck its snout in her coat pocket.

"Sorry, girl, I didn't' bring any treats," she giggled, unable to stop herself from hugging the wet pig.

The pig grunted and stood calmly beside her.

"I'm off on an expedition," Sam chattered nervously. "I'm going to dig for treasure, but don't tell anyone. I think I saw a coin in the mud. That weird crazy looking dude missed it. Do you want to join me?"

The pig snorted and lifted her head, her great belly wobbling with the effort.

"Come on then," Sam chirruped as she shone the flashlight over the narrow trail and walked bravely into the woods.

Gertrude sniffed the air, found nothing that interested her, spun around, and joined the little girl on her adventure.

Sam was ever so glad the pot-bellied pig was with her. She doubted any wild sheep or goats would bother her with Gertrude by her side. The pig was better than a dog, except for Brutus. He was super cool. If Daddy ever let her get a puppy, she decided she'd ask him for a Saint Bernard.

The little girl in the over-sized raincoat and floppy hat crept through the forest. It wasn't long before she stumbled upon the first of a dozen or more holes of varying depth where past treasure hunters had searched for Brother Twelve's long-lost hidden stash of double eagle gold coins.

She scanned the ground; not sure which excavation was the one she was looking for. They all looked the same in the dark.

"Gertrude, do you remember which hole Brutus was digging in," she asked the wayward pig, resting an arm on the top of her shovel.

The pot-bellied pig strolled past her and slid down a hill into the largest of the excavations. It had rained torrents in the late afternoon and the bottom of the hole was awash with mud. The pig slithered into it and laid down, letting out a giant fart as she did so. A geyser of mud burst upward.

"Oh, you goof-ball, you aren't being helpful at all," Sam huffed.

Sam shone her flashlight around the surrounding area. The flashlight's beam illuminated a bunch of snaky looking tree roots.

"Gertrude, you're brilliant," she chimed. "If that is the hole the player was concentrating on, then the hole Brutus was in is this one."

Sam tiptoed over to the tree roots, careful not to fall lest she end up wallowing in the mud alongside Gertrude.

She shone the light on the braid of inky colored roots, tracing their path around to the other side of the tree's base. The giant dog's paw prints were visible in the shallow earth, the thick fir's limbs keeping the base of the tree dry. Something glittered between the forks of a particularly gnarly root.

Sam bent down and plucked the gold coin from the slick earth. She wiped the dirt off on her coat and shone the flashlight on it. The coin was a 1923 gold American double eagle.

"Woohoo," she shouted, forgetting herself. "This must be worth a hundred dollars, maybe even more."

Sam turned out her coat's pockets, making sure that there were no ragged seams or holes, and then pushed the material back inside. She tucked the gold coin inside the deepest pocket, propped the flashlight on the bank so that it was facing down, and then began to dig.

Where there was one gold coin, there must be more, Sam reasoned, unwittingly echoing Morris' thoughts of that afternoon.

Gertrude rolled over and bathed the other side of her body in the gloriously rich mud.

Sam dug for about a half hour, carefully sifting through the dirt to make sure she didn't miss anything. She found no more coins or mason jars filled with loot like Also had described, but she wasn't disappointed. The gold double eagle was there, inside her pocket, proving that she was indeed a true Nicholas, pirate of the high seas.

"Think if I rub the coin, it will give me good luck," she asked the pot-bellied pig.

Gertrude grunted.

A cow mooed sadly somewhere in the dark.

Gertrude squealed, heaved herself upright and scrambled out of nature's bathtub for vivacious pigs. She lumbered into the night.

"Gertrude," Sam shouted, suddenly afraid. "Come back."

Sam struggled to her feet, grabbed the flashlight, and waved it back and forth. The forest was so thick, it swallowed the light. The flashlight's beam faltered. Blackness descended upon the girl like a kidnapper dropping a bag over her head. She slapped the flashlight against one palm, and then shook it vigorously. She fought down the scream that rose to her lips. The light popped back on.

The cow bawled again.

Sam raced after the pig.

Fear gripped her. The forest felt like it was closing in on her, tree limbs snagged at her sleeves, tree roots tried to trip her up. She swore it was on purpose.

Gertrude bulldozed her way through the brush ahead of her. The pig's passage was easy to trace. Sam simply followed the sound.

Sam's flashlight reflected off a piece of plastic. She halted abruptly, her chest heaving, her breath hot against the cold air. The beam of light flicked over the plastic covered windows of the ancient cabin. She let the sabre of light rove over the silver logs, the broken door where a pot-bellied pig stood blocking the entry, and then upwards to the roof where two thin legs were visible.

Sam shrieked!

The flashlight beam wavered. Dark brown velvety eyes, a black muzzle, and a beautiful, serene face stared down at her. Peaches stood on the sod hut's roof, grazing on the last of the green grasses before the snow came.

"Peaches get down from there," the girl scolded the Jersey cow. "You'll break a leg if you go through that roof."

The cow grazed away, oblivious to the child's words of warning.

Sam huffed in disgust. She propped her shovel against a tree and marched around the side of the cabin. She crawled hand over hand up a rock incline until she was level with the Jersey cow.

"Come on, Peaches," she motioned to the cow.

The cow ignored her.

"This is really dumb," she muttered as she cautiously stepped onto the sodden earth. The roof creaked ominously but held her weight.

"Well, if it can hold you, I guess it can hold me," she said through gritted teeth.

Sam inched her way forward, arms out in front of her, until her hand brushed against the cow's neck. She grabbed hold of the tuft of hair on the cow's forehead and clucked.

Peaches reluctantly turned towards the girl, allowing Sam to lead her back to firmer ground.

"You two sure know how to get into trouble," Sam fumed, hands on her hips.

Gertrude walked towards her and nuzzled against her side after Sam returned to earth. Sam couldn't help but laugh. The pig nudged the cow as if giving it a talking to.

"Let's go back to the house," Sam continued with a shake of her head.

Oh, those crazy animals, she giggled.

Well, she had found one gold coin, she reasoned as she struggled to find her way back to the road, the pig and cow ambling along behind her.

Sam fingered the coin inside her pocket, totally forgetting about the shovel she had left behind.

She couldn't wait to show the gold coin to her father.

***

The first job had gone swimmingly, Chris thought. No alarm. No issues. The family left for dinner, or a movie, or wherever it was, they had gone, leaving a side window open. Good for him; bad for them.

Chris had thought the job a bust at first. He moved swiftly, checking the usual places to stash cash and jewels: the icebox, inside a woman's sanitary napkins box, inside a book in the bookcase, but he had come up empty. There wasn't even one necklace or a set of earrings in the parents' bedroom or the little girl's room. No Christmas decorations. No presents. No Christmas cards anywhere.

It didn't faze Chris. Not everyone believed in the holiday. Everyone had jewelry though, didn't they? That puzzled him.

Undeterred, he peeled off his Santa suit and popped it in the dryer for a few minutes. The break-in went so smoothly that he was pretty sure he had the time. If the gig were a bust, then at least he could make use of the facilities. It was a wet row to shore.

Chris hopped into the shower. The scalding water was invigorating.

The athletic thief stepped out of the shower only to discover there weren't any clean towels. He walked naked through the house, rifling through drawers looking for a towel, when a tiny brown envelope fell from the top of one drawer. There was grey duct tape wrapped around the edge.

Chris opened the envelope and burst out laughing. Inside was one hundred, one hundred-dollar bills. He upended the drawers in both bathrooms and the master bedroom, two more envelopes fell to the floor, each with five thousand dollars in one hundred-dollar bills inside.

He was in such high spirits that he decided to at least leave the family breakfast even though his stomach rumbled with hunger. They had been so generous after all.

Chris pulled on his trousers and t-shirt and retrieved his red velvet cloak and pants from the drier. They were still damp but were immensely drier than when he arrived. He popped them on, tugged on his gumboots, and left through the back door, a spring in his step.

"Ho, ho, ho," he mumbled happily.

Chris whistled as he chugged along the inner harbor, looking for another house to hit. Lady Luck was with him. He was on a roll, baby.

Chris saw the rancher that he had cased earlier that morning. There was nobody around. The windows were dark. It looked like the owners were away.

He dropped the anchor, mooring the catamaran far enough from shore that it wouldn't be noticeable yet close enough to row to in a hurry. He devoured a peanut butter sandwich to quell his hunger.

He smiled.

Sam would be so happy when she saw the envelopes filled with cash. If this house wound up a good haul too, he'd head back to Seal Island in the morning.

He liked Seal Island. It was small, remote, but not too remote. People could only access it by boat or the bi-weekly ferry. Best of all, there were empty summer cottages everywhere. He would investigate those in due course. They had time so long as Sam stuck to their story.

Chris rowed to shore and tied the dinghy to the house's narrow wooden dock. The tide was in. This made things easy-peasy.

He looked through the back door and saw an alarm box. The light was red; the security system was alarmed. It looked to be an old alarm system. Once again, good for him, bad for the homeowner.

He popped the deadlock out with one quick seasoned go. He quickly opened the door, raced to the alarm panel, and disabled the alarm. In his haste, he didn't notice the back-up alarm system blinking or the red lights pop on in the cameras placed strategically around the house.

Chris had just stepped into the master bedroom when he heard an outside door bang open. He heard footfalls in the kitchen. Someone besides him was in the house. For the first time in a long time, Chris had neglected to take his boots off. It turned out to be a good thing.

"Hey," a man shouted angrily from the living room. "The cops are on the way, jerk!"

Muffled footsteps raced towards him.

Chris yanked open the bedroom window, sliced through the

screen with a utility knife, and jumped out. He tumbled to the ground, picked himself up, and ran for the boat, gumboots and Santa jacket flapping.

"Busted, Santa," the man screamed, shaking a fist at him through the open window. "You're on camera!"

Chris raced for the dinghy. He just made it to the boat as police cars spun into the yard, red and white lights flashing, sirens silent.

Must be a donut shop close by, Chris laughed dryly.

If not for the eager beaver neighbor trying to be a hero, he'd be in handcuffs in the back seat of a police cruiser by now.

The red suited Santa jumped into the dinghy, untied the line, and cast off. He was surprisingly agile for what was supposed to be a jolly old fat man.

By the time the cops realized the thief had escaped in a rowboat, it was too late.

Santa's dinghy clanged against the sides of the catamaran. Chris had made it there in record time. It was almost as if dolphins had replaced the reindeer pulling Santa's sled. He climbed aboard, raised the rowboat, and quickly hauled anchor.

With running lights dark, Chris putted slowly out of the harbor and out into open sea. The wind had picked up enough that Chris raised the main sail.

He saw a police boat sweep into the harbor the catamaran had just vacated, but by then he was under sail and sweeping across the water, back towards Seal Island, the catamaran gliding stealthily away to safety.

The main sail snapped.

The wind blew steadily at twenty knots.

Chris tacked to leeward.

He laughed as the wind caught the sails and the catamaran skipped into top gear. He tugged off the floppy red hat and the long white beard.

"Caught on camera," he grinned. "What're you going to do? Arrest every mall Santa in the area?"

Chris gleefully made his way back to his daughter, a cool

twenty thousand dollars in the cupboard above his bunk.

Double Trouble

December 13th – afternoon

Pearl sat on the back porch wrapped in a winter coat, a colorful hand knit shawl over her lap, drinking a cup of English Breakfast tea. There were two empty teacups in front of two empty chairs across the table for the ghosts of her two friends, Tammy Smith, and Summer River, should they choose to join her. In the center of the table was another teacup on a saucer, turned upside down, and a full pot of tea, a honey jar with a wooden spoon, and a small milk jug.

The morning was misty, fog hung low over the road. Water dripped from trees.

Large red and gold maple leaves covered her flower beds. Layers of straw toppled over the sides of the raised vegetable garden planters.

Despite the dampness, and her nagging arthritis, Pearl enjoyed sitting there listening to the silence.

She saw a dapper figure walking down the road, wrapped in a long trench coat and sporting a French hat.

"Top of the morning to you, Also," Pearl waved at the jaunty lad. "That's a mighty fine raspberry beret that you are wearing."

Also stopped at the garden gate and lifted a hand in a half-hearted wave.

Something was wrong. Also wasn't his normal cheery self. The hat that Also was wearing was very familiar. She should know. It was her deceased friend's Tammy's favorite fall hat.

"Thank-you Miss Pearl," Also croaked. "It is a fine hat. My friend Sam gave it to me."

That was odd, Pearl mused.

Who was Sam and why did she give Also Tammy's hat?

"Why don't you come in and have a biscuit with jam," Pearl waved the young man forward. "I just opened a fresh jar of strawberry jam this morning."

Also looked down at his feet and thought for a moment. He looked so sad, Pearl thought. What was going on?

"Also, are you all right," she asked worriedly.

"Also isn't feeling well today," the boy sighed.

"Come sit with me," Pearl replied, patting the chair beside her. "A cup of tea will help with that, not to mention a friend to talk to."

Also beamed and opened the garden gate. He trudged through the garden and onto the covered patio.

"Sit here," Pearl commanded, pointing to the chair beside her.

"But that's Miss Tammy's chair," the boy wailed.

"It's yours today," Pearl ventured, pouring the pale faced teen a cup of tea. "Now help yourself to honey and milk."

Also smiled at Pearl. It was such a tragic smile that it broke her heart break.

"Has something happened to upset you," Pearl asked.

"No, I just don't feel candy apple happy today," Also sighed, adding a double helping of honey to his cup of tea.

"Well," Pearl replied, "why don' you tell me about your friend Sam. Do I know him?"

"Sam's not him, Sam's her," Also grinned, his eyes lighting up. "She's my new friend."

"Ahh, I see, and where does Sam live," Pearl pressed him.

"She lives at the laughing lady's house, but not for long." Also sobbed. "I don't want Sam to go. Also will miss her. He won't have anyone to go treasure hunting with."

Pearl sat back in her chair, her mind buzzing. She knew who Also's laughing lady was. It was Tammy Smith, her long time friend and school mate. Despite the stiffness in her hips and knees, Pearl felt that a walk to Tammy's house was in order. She needed to check out this Sam.

"How is the tea," Pearl queried. "Is it helping you feel better?"

Also nodded and slurped his tea.

"When you're done, why don't we take a walk. I'd like to meet your friend," Pearl remarked casually.

"Maybe Sam has another raspberry beret and we can be twins," Also giggled, cheering up.

Pearl smiled. The boy wasn't looking so pale anymore.

"Knock. Knock," the boy sang.

"Who's there," Pearl grinned.

"Hatch."

"Hatch who," the old woman smiled.

"God bless you," Also chimed.

Pearl and Also laughed heartily.

"I think maybe I can eat a biscuit and jam now," he said.

Now Pearl knew the young man was feeling better.

***

Morris strode out of the bush, his Border collie and the Saint Bernard galloping out of it ahead of him. His orangey-red beard bounced off his red and black lumberjack shirt. His gumboots were thick with mud. He carried a short-handled shovel in one hand.

Morris' face was as bleak as the day. He suspected it was the girl who had been digging around the prophet's cabin. That was tantamount to trying to claim-jump a gold miner, in his opinion.

Morris reached the laneway to Tammy Smith's house. The side gate was open. There were fresh cow pies in the front yard and cloven hoof prints everywhere. Gertrude and Peaches had done a fine job of cleaning out the garden.

The goat farmer snorted in amusement. The pair was running amok with Betty and Reggie gone. Archie and Vi weren't on top of it. He'd have to start shutting the gate to his property.

Morris banged on the cottage's front door.

A child's hand pulled the curtain aside in the living room and then let the curtain fall back into place. The troublesome girl was definitely inside the house.

Morris knocked even harder.

"Come on, girlie, I know yer in there," he growled.

Still no response.

Morris lifted the shovel and used the handle as a battering ram.

***

Sam stood at the door on her tippy toes looking through the peep hole. She was still in her pajamas. They were flannel with blue sailing boats and black anchors on an ivory background. They were boy's pajamas, but Sam loved them all the same. She wasn't a 'frilly' kind of girl.

Through the peep hole, she watched the goat farmer's face get redder and redder. He looked like a Disney cartoon. She wondered when he was going to blow up. She could have sworn she saw smoke coming out of his ears.

His beard and hair poked out sideways from beneath a tattered ball cap. The ball cap was so worn, the emblem was unreadable.

The shovel that Morris was using to try to break down the door looked familiar.

Bang. Bang. Bang.

The door frame shuddered but held fast.

Sam raced to the back door to double check it was locked. She didn't want the crazy guy to come around back and simply walk into the house. Daddy didn't raise a dummy.

The front door frame shook even harder.

Sam wished her daddy were here.

"What is all that racket," her father growled, striding down the hallway from the direction of the master bedroom.

"Daddy! You are home," Sam shrieked, throwing herself into his arms.

"I came home late last night," he hugged her. "I didn't want to wake you. Now, what is going on?"

"There's a crazy man out there," she shivered. "I met him in the woods yesterday with my friend, Also."

"Who is Also? And what were you doing in the woods," he

thundered over the ear-shattering banging on the front door.

"Tell you later," Sam trembled, recoiling from her father's anger.

Wait until Daddy sees the coin I found, she thought, gnawing on a strand of coal colored hair. *I bet he'll do the Snoopy- dance with me.*

Her father yanked open the door, his face stiff, his body set in what Sam thought of as his 'don't mess with me' stance.

"Who're you," Morris demanded, taking a step backwards.

"Sam's father. What do you think you're doing?" Chris fumed.

Morris' Border collie, Max, who had been sniffing around in the garden, looked up. He took one look at Chris Nicholas and bolted for home.

The Saint Bernard rolled in a pile of cow dung, coating each side of his glorious coat with brownish green sludge.

Sam peeked out from behind her father, saw the filthy dog, and tried unsuccessfully to smother a giggle.

"Morris Tweedsmuir," the goat farmer stuttered, his eyes narrowing as he saw the laughing girl standing behind her father.

"Yer daughter was poking her nose where it don't belong and left this behind," Morris seethed, lifting the shovel.

"Is that your shovel, honey," Chris calmly asked his daughter.

"Nope, not mine," his daughter replied with a shake of her head.

"There you have it," Chris sneered.

"Morris Tweedsmuir stop hassling our new neighbors," an old woman yelled as she approached the house. Beside the white-haired woman draped in one of the most beautiful rainbow-colored shawls that Sam had ever seen walked her friend, Also.

Sam waved at Also.

Also waved back.

"That's my friend Also, Daddy," she whispered.

Sam saw her father scan the strapping young lad in the funny overcoat with a red lady's beret perched jauntily on one side of his head, a cherubic grin on his face, and grunted in response.

Sam didn't understand.

She thought Daddy would be happy that she made a friend.

"Pearl," Morris greeted her. "Also. What're you doing out walking about on such a chilly day?"

"Why I'm coming to greet our new neighbors and drop off a jar of jam and some homemade biscuits," Pearl replied smoothly, pulling a jar of jam and a baggie of fresh biscuits from out of her coat pocket. "That's what good neighbors do."

Morris harrumphed in response.

"Looks like Brutus needs a bath," Also laughed.

"It does so," Pearl ventured, amused.

The dog bounced out of the garden and over to Also. Also ran away from the dog, holding his nose closed with two fingers. The dog thought it was great fun and raced after the young man.

"Let me introduce myself," Pearl continued. "I'm Pearl Tullis and you are?"

"Sorry, where's my manners," Chris grinned, turning on the charm. "I'm Chris Nicholas and this is my daughter, Sam. We're only here for a few days. The estate's lawyer asked me to check on the house and do some clean up."

"By the look of the yard, I'd say that Gertie and Peaches have done that for you," Pearl grinned, walking up to the door, her walking cane making a rickety-tick sound on the cobblestone path. She held out the jar of jam and the package of biscuits.

Sam coyly accepted the gifts. The old lady reminded Sam of the fairy godmother in her book, Snow White. Her eyes were so warm, they lit her face up like a firecracker.

"Who are Gertie and Peaches?"

"The local color," Pearl chortled.

"Gertrude's a pot-bellied pig and Peaches is a cow," Sam explained to her father. "They're my friends too."

"I expect Also will be back to help you eat those biscuits once he gets away from Brutus," the woman joked.

Sam smiled.

"I think that might be awhile yet," Chris chuckled as he watched the boy run circle eights in the street, trying to keep the slobbering dog at bay.

"Nah, I'll go fetch my dog," Morris grumbled.

Morris stamped the shovel's blade into the soft earth, glared at Sam, and stalked off, leaving the evidence of Sam's adventure behind.

"Don't mind, Morris, he's all bark," Pearl smirked. "He's a good man normally. He's just angry that his sister has run back to the city with her beau instead of returning to college. Can't blame her. That boyfriend of hers is a handsome so-and-so."

"Well, thank you for the lovely treats," Chris schmoozed. "I'd ask you in, but as you can see, my daughter is still in her pjs and I've only just got up myself."

"Not a problem," Pearl nodded. "I live in the yellow cottage with the white trim and picket fence down the street. You are welcome to visit any time."

"Thank you," Sam squeaked, liking the woman.

"It looks like you may need to rescue that poor boy," Chris noticed.

"Oh dear," Pearl said, looking down the road to where the Saint Bernard was dragging Morris down the road, tail wagging furiously as Also tried to keep out of the manure covered happy-go-lucky giant puppy's grasp.

Pearl hustled off the porch towards the melee.

"Don't let that dog knock you over, Mrs Tullis," Chris warned her.

Pearl lifted her cane in response and puttered down the road.

"I'll see you later, Also," Sam shouted.

"No, you won't," Sam's father replied flatly.

"What were you thinking," he scolded his daughter as he closed the door. "Do you want me to get busted? Do you want to end up in a foster home? You think it would be fun visiting dear old daddy in prison?"

"I'm sorry," Sam stammered, crestfallen.

"You know better, Sam! I suggest you get some sleep," he grumbled, wandering off to the kitchen. "Since I can't trust you to behave when I'm gone, you're going to have to come with me tonight."

"Can I go on the job with you," she squeaked, deciding now was not the time to tell her father about the gold coin she found.

"Maybe," he relented, plugging in the kettle.

"Can I wear my elf clothes," she grinned.

Chris burst out laughing and then kissed her on the cheek.

"How about we have biscuits and jam and then we'll discuss whether you can wear your elf suit tonight."

Sam grabbed a couple of plates from the cupboard. The jam and biscuits looked delicious.

One bite had her melting like butter. The biscuits were soft and moist, positively scrumptious in her opinion. She ladled jam onto the next and bit into it. Jam dripped down her chin.

Whether Daddy liked it or not, she was not going to give up Also as a friend, and she was not going to not visit the old lady with the incredible biscuits, even if it meant going to a foster home.

***

The Persephone pulled out of the marina at Alert Bay, a native fishing village nestled amongst the snow topped peaks of the northern coastal mountains of British Columbia. It was as quaint a spot as one could imagine, the locals shouting 'hellos' to the newlyweds wherever they went.

A kind-hearted soul had offered up a brown leather harness that fit Mugsy as if it had been custom made for him.

The pug was doing much better now that it had a chance to rest and a full stomach. The dog was still over needy, but both Reggie and Betty knew that was to be expected.

Betty thought her husband was amazing, taking everything in stride, including the growls that came from the rescued dog every time that he got close to Betty.

The couple had picked up some basic supplies and then Reggie's friend's wife had presented them with some maple sugar smoked salmon, a jar of local honey, and two jars of pickled Oolichan smelts. Reggie loved the pickled Oolichan, but they were a bit oily for Betty's liking. The woman had also given them a couple of frozen pink salmon for the dogs. Betty was touched by the kindness of the gesture.

The Phoenixes only stayed in port for a few hours as Reggie seemed anxious to show her the sights. She had never been this far up the coast and it was already proving to be an adventure. It was abundantly clear that her husband was well known and well liked.

As she waved at everyone lined up on the docks to see them off, she felt a wave of foreboding sweep over her. She didn't know why. The boat was well stocked. Her husband was a seasoned sailor. They were on the honeymoon trip of a lifetime, one that few people in the world would ever make, yet still she felt as if they should turn around and head back into more populated waters.

The sun broke out of the clouds causing the fog to dissipate. It was a beautiful winter's day. The inland mountains were covered in snow, but the forest along the waterline was lush and green.

Betty shrugged and snuggled with the pug in her arms. Champ whined, sensing his master's unease, and leaned against her leg. Betty absently rubbed behind his ear.

I'm just tired, Betty sighed.

They had been on the go since they tied the knot and for days before as well. Once they moored inside the Conservancy, they would drop anchor and stay for a few days. Betty held onto that thought as she turned her face towards the sun.

Fire in the Sky

December 13th – night

Reggie and Betty relaxed in lounge chairs on the deck of *The Persephone*, throw rugs tucked around their legs, a bottle of merlot resting on the wood planking between them. Mugsy was tucked safely inside a fleecy blanket on Betty's lap. The shepherd was curled on top of a fleece lined dog bed beside Reggie.

Stars twinkled overhead.

Wavering green lights flickered over the northern tip of the mainland, shifting in a kaleidoscope of swirling waves as the Northern Lights danced across the sky.

The weather had held for their trip up the coast, but the change was already in progress as a thick layer of clouds scuttled towards the trawler. A layer of fog gathered in the narrows close to where they were moored. It wouldn't be long before the swirling mists engulfed them.

A blazing meteor ripped across the sky, plunging to earth in a heavenly shower of sparks.

"Ooh, did you see that one, honey," Betty gasped in delight.

"I did," Reggie grinned. "Look, there's another."

The pair were awestruck as the meteor shower and Northern Lights continued to bedazzle the night sky.

All good things must come to an end. The fog rolled in a half hour later. It was as thick as molasses. The light show was over for everyone but the crew and passengers on the planes that flew high above the clouds.

"I'll put away the chairs and wine glasses," Reggie said, standing up. "You look after the pups."

"All right, honey," Betty answered, downing the last of the

wine in her glass. She handed the glass to her husband, bent over and placed the pug down on the deck, much to the dog's disagreement.

Betty wandered across the deck to the boat's stern. Reggie had laid an artificial grass mat down so that the dogs could do their business when they couldn't go ashore. Champ went directly over to the carpet and cocked a leg. The pug looked up in disgust.

"Go on, I'm not waiting all night. It's cold out here," she quipped staring the pug down.

Betty wrapped the throw rug around her shoulders. The air was getting chillier by the minute.

Champ whined, the hair on his back rising.

"What's wrong, partner," she asked the big shepherd.

The German shepherd had come into her life two years earlier. He had been a timid dog when she first met him, but they had bonded instantly, much in the same way as the pug did with her at the beach. Champ had proven his worth many times since then. Even though Betty was semi-retired, law enforcement was in her blood. She knew she would probably never completely retire, and neither would her four-legged partner.

The shepherd whimpered and walked stiffly over to the port side. The damp chill was affecting him too. A long, threatening growl rose from deep inside his throat.

The pug peed on the spot.

Betty scooped the little dog up and searched the water.

"What's the matter with Champ," Reggie asked, sauntering across the deck, the half full bottle of wine dangling from one hand.

"Dunno," she replied.

The dog growled again.

A row of red lights bobbed towards them in the fog. The rumble of a diesel engine filled the night.

They had moored The Persephone with only the red running lights on the bow and stern alight, but the LED lights in the cabin reflected off the water through the portal windows down below. The fog was so thick, the lower deck lights looked like the yellowed headlights of an old car. A single LED lit up the wheel-house.

This wasn't a main thorough fare, and it was off season, so Reggie had gone minimalist to better view the stars.

"Strange that they'd be running like that at this time of night," Reggie hissed. "They should glow like a Christmas tree."

"Do you think we should light up *The Persephone* so they can see us," Betty whispered, sensing her husband's unease.

"I'll light her up if I needs ta," he mumbled, his eyes fixed upon the other boat's passage. Its current course would take it danger-ously close to them.

Betty moved closer to her husband. His body was tense, his jaw rigid.

"You're making me nervous," she trembled.

"Hmmm," he grunted.

This isn't good, Betty thought, her hand instinctively going to the side where her revolver used to be. She shifted the dog in her arms.

"Don't ya go barking, Champ," Reggie warned the shepherd. "Let's all be quiet like. I'll flip on our running lights and blow a horn if'n I need ta. We still got time."

The dog crowded the old fisherman. It stood at attention, ears forward, eyes alert, one paw resting on his boot.

The silhouette of a large seiner drifted by with barely a ripple of water, going so slow as to be unseen except for the soft glow of its intermittent running lights and the muffled chug of the large diesel engine as it passed.

Betty shivered. It looked like a ghost ship. Portals dark. The bridge shrouded in shadows. The boat drifting silently through the fog. She felt like she was in a horror movie.

"You think they saw us," Betty whispered.

"If'n they did, they aren't interested," he sighed, "and that's a good thing."

"There aren't any pirates in these waters, are there," she fret-ted, wishing she had a gun aboard. Maybe in the future, she would do that.

"Not generally, but there are drug runners in these waters. More than ya'd care to know about," he replied, talking from experience. "People smugglers too, but it's been awhile since I've heard tales of that. Most folks come by airplane now and don't bother leaving, but that's yer expertise, not mine."

"I've never worked narcotics or immigration," she confessed, "only major crimes. I remember that migrant ship that went aground on the west coast years ago, though. As for smugglers, that one's on you, my love."

"Anyway, they're gone now, so let's pack it in," he grinned, referring to his past life as a minor league pot smuggler. "I can think of other things I'd rather be doing than standing out here in the cold."

Betty laughed lightly. He was trying to make her feel better. That was funny in a sexy kind of damsel in distress kind of way. Her husband was more Don Quixote than King Arthur, though.

As they made their way back to the cabin, the shepherd hung back.

"I think we should leave Champ in the wheelhouse tonight," Reggie noted, noticing the dog's reluctance to leave its post.

"Yeah, I think that's a good idea," she agreed. "Maybe we'll sleep better."

"Don't worry about that, sweetie," he chortled. "I'll make sure yer good and tired."

"Promises, promises," Betty teased him back, knowing that she'd be sleeping with one eye open.

***

Sam yanked on the emerald green stockings and tunic they found in a costume shop last year. The tunic was a little tight since she had grown a good six inches since then. She tugged on the pointy forest green hat that completed the ensemble. Daddy had sewn a fake blond wig into the hat to hide her black hair.

Sam was excited. She hadn't been on a job with her father in ages.

"Ready, honey," the skinny Santa Claus in the doorway asked.

"Almost," Sam grinned, reaching for the burgundy-colored velvet bag sitting on her bed.

Santa-daddy gave her a thumbs up.

Sam followed her dad onto the deck and then climbed into the rowboat. She settled herself on the front seat and looked up at the stars. It was a magnificent night.

A falling star shot across the sky.

"Quick, make a wish," Chris told his daughter.

Sam gasped and made her wish: *I wish to find more buried treasure and for daddy to be proud of me.*

Another meteor shot across the horizon.

"Wow, Daddy, look at them all," the girl marveled.

"It's good luck," her father grinned. "We're going to have a great night, sweetie."

Sam sat in the dinghy, her neck straining as she stared upwards, her mouth open, her eyes bright with wonder, as her father rowed to shore.

The water sloshed against the two-seater dinghy as they rowed up to the long dock in front of the first of their jobs. Sam reached for the rubber bumper that kept boats from slamming into the dock, found a tie-down, and slipped a rope around it, while her father tucked the oars in beside the seat. They were hitting cottages on Denman Island tonight instead of the main island.

"We're going to the cottage on the right first," he said as he helped her out of the boat.

"Okay," she responded, skipping away, the dock rocking gently beneath her sneakers.

Her father hummed a familiar tune behind her as they climbed up the stone steps to the first cottage. It was *Bridge Over Troubled Water* by Simon and Garfunkel. Her daddy loved that tune.

The A-frame cottage atop the slope in front of them was lifeless. It looked sad and forlorn against the meteor and star-studded sky.

Her father used his tools to break into the house. He then held the door open for her like a proper gentleman.

Sam grinned.

While her dad rifled through the bedrooms, Sam checked out the kitchen cupboards and pantry. She flashed her little penlight around, looking for goodies or hiding places for cash that might be over-looked such as inside coffee tins and pasta holders.

She then helped herself to some cans of tuna, five boxes of Kraft dinner, and two packages of Oreo cookies, tossing them into the bag depending on their expiry date. The people that owned the cottage weren't very careful. Daddy had taught her how to check for expiry dates on cans after they got sick once from eating outdated pea soup. That was a yucky experience. She wanted to leave the homeowners a note telling them that they should clean out their pantry, but that would be silly. It was their problem anyway.

There wasn't much in the fridge, so the folks that owned the cottage probably weren't coming back this year.

It was a little disappointing, but you can't win them all.

Her father returned quickly. He stalked around the house like a rangy tomcat. Sam could tell he was both angry and disappointed.

Yep, it was a bust, she thought as he motioned for her to join him.

The second house looked more promising. It was a much larger house than the A-frame. It was two stories high and had a built-in propane fireplace on the deck. Red cushions adorned the wicker furniture. Sam could imagine having dinner with her new friend, Also, and Daddy there. Maybe they could have pork chops. In Sam's opinion, you could never eat enough pork chops and mashed potatoes.

There was a light on over the kitchen stove. Sam was about to point it out to her father when he turned the handle on the back door, and the door sprung open.

"Huh," he mumbled. "It's not locked."

He strode inside the house before Sam could warn him.

Sam scurried into the house after him, all her senses tingling.

She felt like spiderman. Okay, maybe not spiderman since she wore an elf costume, but close enough.

"I'll go up, you stay down," her father whispered, pocketing his flashlight.

Sam didn't turn hers on either because the light over the stove lit up the kitchen and the front living room.

Maybe she was wrong, maybe her daddy had the same feeling as her… they weren't alone.

Sam watched her father creep up the stairs. He disappeared down a hall, so Sam turned around and went to check out the Christmas tree in the living room. It was only half decorated. She picked up a red and gold dewdrop decoration. Her fake blond hair reflected in the glass, her cheeks looking even rosier than normal. Sam smiled, wrapped the glass bauble in some tissue paper and carefully tucked it inside her pocket.

Sam then went into the kitchen and silently rifled through all the drawers and containers on the counter. Two twenty-dollar bills and a tenner were wrapped in a tight bundle beneath a tea cannister. The bills went into her pocket.

Sam opened the fridge and discovered a turkey. It sat on the lower rack defrosting. The turkey was so big that nothing else could fit in the fridge.

It took two hands for Sam to lift the bird.

Her father rushed around the corner.

"Time to go," was all he said.

"Look, Christmas dinner," she wheedled.

Chris smirked, lifted the turkey one armed out of the fridge and dumped it inside his own sack.

"Come on," he whispered fiercely. "We aren't alone. I don't care if I get caught, but I don't want you going to juvie."

Sam's eyes widened. Her heart skipped a beat.

She darted out of the house, running as fast as she could to keep up with her father, down the swaying dock and into the dinghy.

A light popped on in the cottage as they rowed away. A woman screamed. Her shriek echoed across the water. An angry man in pink silk pajamas jogged down the stairs. The man then raced to the back door and out into the yard.

What kind of man wears pink silk pajamas?

Sam and her daddy were too far away for pink pajama guy to see them. That was good. She didn't fancy meeting him.

"That was too close for comfort," Chris hissed when they returned to the catamaran.

"But we didn't get nabbed," Sam chirped, trying to cheer her father up.

Chris tugged off his beard and hat and tossed them angrily to the bottom of the boat.

"And we got Christmas dinner," her voice warbled, picking up the Santa hat and beard so they didn't get wet.

"We did that," her father agreed, his mood lightening. He playfully tugged at her jester hat.

"Where are we going next," Sam smiled.

"Back to Seal Island. They've probably called the cops, so we'll hightail it back to the cottage."

"Oh, okay," she sighed, trying to sound disappointed.

"Sorry about that kiddo," her father sighed.

"It wasn't a total waste of time," she crowed, handing him the fifty dollars from her pocket.

"Where d'you find this," he cheered.

"Under the tea cannister," Sam beamed.

"Impressive," he chuckled. "Now let's get under way."

Sam helped her father pull the dinghy up and weigh anchor. Before she knew it, they were underway, heading back to Seal Island and Tammy Smith's cottage.

It had been fun, and she loved being on the water, but Sam was secretly happy. She got to go on a job with her dad, and she found the most amazing turkey. They hadn't ever cooked a turkey that big before.

The little girl carefully tugged the Christmas glass ornament out of her pocket as she went down below. She let it spin on the end of the string. It was the prettiest thing she had ever seen.

This was going to be the greatest Christmas ever.

***

Betty awoke from a fitful sleep to the sound of Champ's frantic barking and a howl of pain.

Reggie jumped out of bed and was instantly knocked unconscious by the butt of a rifle.

Two men grabbed hold of her and dragged her out of bed, bending her arms backwards and tying them with zip ties. The plastic zip ties bit into her wrist's tender flesh.

The pug went flying, yipping in pain as it bounced off a wall.

Reggie was subdued the same way.

It was all over in less than a minute.

"Reggie," she cried worriedly.

Her husband groaned as he was hauled out of bed and through the wheelhouse.

"Get up," one of her attackers yelled at her.

He kicked her in the side when she didn't respond fast enough. Betty bit back the retort that came to her lips. Fear caught her in a stranglehold. She wasn't afraid for herself. She was scared for her husband and her dogs.

Was her husband okay?

Was the shepherd alive?

Would Mugsy survive a toss like that?

Her police training kicked into high gear. Survey. Plan. Survive. Don't panic, being the keywords. That was what she told herself.

Betty struggled to her feet, which was harder than she realized with her hands tied behind her back.

The other attacker wasn't so violent. He helped her up the stairs to the upper deck.

She sighed with relief when she saw Champ muzzled and tied to the railing by a short chain. Her little pug limped up the stairs and cowered beside her.

"Hey, little guy," the nicer of the attackers said, holding out a hand to the pug.

Mugsy promptly bit him.

Betty silently cheered the old dog on.

"Little shite is more like it," the man who kicked her growled.

Undeterred, the short haired wiry attacker held out a piece of salmon jerky. Unable to help itself, the pug darted forwards into the man's waiting arms and gobbled down the piece of jerky.

Betty inhaled sharply, pain rippling through her wrists and upper arms, as two powerful hands lifted her to her feet, and then tossed her unceremoniously against the ship's railings. Crack! Her back exploded in pain.

She was then tied to the railing beside her German shepherd with more zip ties. Champ whined and tried to lick her hand but couldn't because of the muzzle.

Two men dragged Reggie's still unconscious form over to the rail and tied him beside Betty.

At least her husband was still breathing. The knot on his forehead was already the size of a goose egg. That wasn't good. Reggie probably had a concussion.

She heard the splash of oars in the water and muffled voices drifting towards her. They weren't speaking in English, so she didn't know what the people were saying. Two rowboats pulled up to the stern. They were overflowing with Asian faces, mostly families. The women and girls wore head coverings, which was odd.

The men and women looked as shell shocked as she felt, downtrodden, unable to look up. They shuffled off the boats.

One man wore a round hat and carried a small book in his hands. It looked like a bible or prayer book. His hands were gnarled, his face lined from years in the sun. The man wasn't as afraid as the others. He looked her square in the eye and then turned to one of the smugglers, whispering something in his ear.

The smuggler glanced warily in Betty's direction, nodded, and turned back to the silver haired older man. The Asian smuggler assisted the older man into the hold.

Dear God, they are human traffickers, she realized, searching the faces of the mostly Caucasian crew.

Then it donned on her. These people must be Muslim Chinese.

She had read about their plight. Uighurs, she thought sadly.

But what were these men smuggling Uighurs in the middle of the night at sea into Canada for? Surely, these people could have applied for asylum through regular channels.

Here they were though, right in front of her, being led like cattle onto *The Persephone* and down into the hold. At least the boat's hold hadn't been used for storing fish for years. Reggie had built racks for scuba diving gear and a portable shop. He had given up his fishing license ten years ago.

"How many more," the thin man holding Betty's pug asked one of the crew.

"One more boat load. You want us to scuttle the seiner," the man replied.

"Nah, it's sinking anyway. It'll look more natural if it goes down on its own. Make sure you don't leave any rowboats behind. I don't want the Coastguard searching for the crew because they found an empty dinghy."

So, that was it. They wanted *The Persephone*, Betty snorted, annoyed. Their ship was sinking. Perhaps it had mechanical problems as well given the lack of lights when it passed them.

She wasn't sure what these men had planned for her and Reggie but doubted it was going to be good.

Still, she kept her silence. No point in aggravating the leader or any of his men.

The short haired boss strode across the deck and stood looking down at her. He said nothing, simply regarded her with a calm detachment that made Betty cringe inside.

He kicked Reggie's foot. Reggie instinctively recoiled, his bare foot pulling up towards his body, but he didn't wake up.

Anger burned inside her. She wanted to channel her inner Gertrude and headbutt the short, little sod.

The smuggler chortled, an amused look creeping over his face.

These men didn't know the coast very well, or they would have known that *The Persephone* was the worst boat imaginable to steal. It was one of a kind, plus its captain was well known. Reggie had friends everywhere. If they thought the black hull made the renovated trawler the perfect smuggling boat, they were in for a big surprise. When Reggie was still managing his own grow-op business, prior to going legit and then selling out his specialty cannabis lines to an international company, the boat had been painted white with blue trim to be as inconspicuous as possible.

Betty almost smiled... almost. She didn't want the smuggler to demand to know what she was smiling about thereby jeopardizing their chance of rescue.

The smuggler patted the pug, the dog seemingly content in his arms.

The crew prodded the last boat load of Chinese families across the deck and down into the dark hold. A child screamed. Its mother rocked the two-year-old in her arms and sang a pretty lullaby. The child quieted.

"That's it," one of the crew shouted.

"Good," the leader said. "What about the dogs?"

"They were on the last boat," the crewman returned. "We had to crate the Pitbull. She ripped into the triad dude."

"Put it in the hold," the leader laughed and turned back to Betty. "Don't give me a reason to toss you overboard and I won't. Well, maybe not. I haven't decided yet."

The man turned and strolled back to the wheelhouse as if he hadn't a care in the world. A Border collie with a white splash like spray paint on its face and speckled legs raced out of the darkness. It slipped between her and Champ, curling itself into as small a ball as possible and glancing around furtively.

The German shepherd whined.

The Border collie sidled up to Champ submissively.

"Shhhh, it'll be all right," she whispered to the dogs.

The Border collie licked her chin.

Betty heard the scrape of the anchor chain as it was hauled aboard. Shortly thereafter, the twin diesel engines coughed into life.

The pilot turned north towards Prince Rupert and cruised slowly out of the bay, chugging along the eastern most channel into a thickening fog.

"Honey, if you can hear me, you need to play dead," she mumbled into Reggie's ear. He moaned ever so softly in response.

The one thing that Betty knew for certain was that the leader had been lying. She had seen his face. He was going to kill them as soon as he found a more out of the way location.

Betty's teeth chattered. She wore a simple cotton nightdress. Her feet were as bare as her husband's. Her toes were turning white from the cold. Reggie was bare chested. She pressed against him for warmth, worried that he would get hypothermia. His skin was warm to the touch and his breathing regular.

He opened one eye, winked at her, and then closed it again.

Oh, you crusty old seadog, she mused with a roll of her eyes.

"Here," the sour faced Asian smuggler who had been talking with the old Chinese man grumbled, tossing a smelly woolen blanket over the two of them. "Boss says too cold."

The man smirked and then stalked away.

That was weird, Betty started. *She thought the thin man who took Mugsy was the boss?*

The Border collie moved over and laid on top of the blanket, snuggling in between her and Reggie. Its nose rubbed up against her chin as the collie sighed with relief. Champ leaned into her back, also seeking comfort and shelter from the elements. The blanket stank like a gym bag, but she was grateful for its warmth.

*** *

Morris Tweedsmuir hunkered down inside Brother Twelve's cabin, a sleeping bag and a camp lantern on the floor beside him. The night was frigid. The door to the cabin lay open. He hadn't wanted to close it lest it bring unwanted attention upon him.

Morris had just turned off the lantern when his cell phone buzzed. It was Pearl Tullis. She had enlisted the aid of Frank and Rainbow McDonald. The catamaran was back in the cove at the back of their farm.

"Told you there's something fishy about that girl and her

father," he said to Pearl, unfurling the sleeping bag and tugging it up to his chin.

"I know, Morris, we already talked about it on the way home this afternoon," the old woman agreed.

The odd boy named Also had taken up a friendship with the girl, and Pearl didn't want to upset him. Even Morris could see that the young man wasn't well. He looked drawn and pale. He'd lost a lot of weight since the summer, too. They both thought it wise to keep their suspicions secret and away from Also's tender ears.

"Gotta go, someone's coming," he whispered, hanging up the phone.

Morris cast the sleeping bag aside.

There were footsteps on the path from the beach. A flashlight's beam reflected off the fog in the meadow.

Father and daughter walked right past him, their gaze intent on the path they were following. They each carried a sack over their shoulder.

Morris wondered what was in those sacks.

The father's looked the heaviest.

"Don't fall in a hole," the man cautioned his daughter.

"I won't," she squeaked.

Morris watched through the broken plastic in the window, his head barely visible above the windowsill.

Gertrude and Peaches jogged up from the beach. The pot-bellied pig raced over to the girl, but the Jersey cow walked straight to the cabin's door, stuck her head inside, and mooed a greeting.

"Get out of here, Peaches," he whispered hoarsely, flicking a hand at the cow as she nosed her way into the cabin.

"What the heck," the man exclaimed, jumping out of the way of the pig.

"Daddy, meet Gertrude. Gertrude, meet Daddy," the girl chirped, wrapping an arm around the pig's neck. "She's my friend."

"What is she doing out here," the man asked worriedly, "especially at this time of night."

He pushed Gertrude's snout roughly aside as he spun around, looking for the pig's owner. The half-frozen twenty-five-pound turkey slammed into her head. The pig squealed in pain.

"Be careful, you hit her," Sam cried out.

Inside the sod hut, Morris found the handle of a broken broom and prodded the cow in the chest. Peaches backed out of the cabin.

"I suppose that cow is your friend too?" Chris barked at his daughter.

"That's Peaches," Sam wailed.

"That's enough," Chris ordered his daughter. "You'll wake the dead."

Morris heard the young girl whimper. She wasn't so tough now, was she?

He squinted through the plastic and saw her throw herself on top of Gertrude as the pig lowered her head and plunge forward, intent on head-butting the girl's father into the treasure hole.

You go, Gertie, he thought, his face breaking into a malicious smile. *Maybe the kid isn't so bad after all?*

The man squealed like... well, like a pig. He jumped behind a tree and screamed at the girl: "Get that thing away from me."

"Stop hurting her and she won't try to hurt you," the girl fumed, hands on her hips.

Gertrude turned towards the girl and nudged her gently. The kid was too small though and fell to the ground.

"Ow," she said, picking herself back up. "I hope you didn't break my Christmas ornament."

The girl plucked what looked like a fiery glass ball out of the bag.

Even from here, Morris could hear her sigh of relief.

What was a kid doing with a Christmas ball in a bag in the woods in the middle of the night?

"Come on, Sam," her father hissed. "It's late. I don't like this. I want to get back to the cottage as fast as possible."

"Yes, Daddy," the girl mumbled, contrite.

The kid kissed Gertrude on the snout and then ran after her

father, flashlight bobbing over the trail. Gertrude watched her go. Peaches wandered over to stand beside her.

Betty really needed to get back to Seal Island in a hurry. Honeymoon be darned. She was needed at home. She would be furious with her father when she found out that Gertrude and Peaches were wandering around in the woods at night, Morris mused.

He shook his head in consternation and rolled up his sleeping bag.

"Gertie," he mumbled, exiting the cabin. "Peaches. Come with me you two."

The pot-bellied pig and cow ambled over to him. Morris gave them both a pat.

When he thought it was safe, Morris lit the lantern and urged the animals to follow him as he marched through the woods heading for the McDonald's farm. He needed to get his two buddies to safety. Hopefully, Rainbow and Frank would lock them up before they got into more trouble.

He smirked. He was right. There was something shady about that Chris fellow. The daughter was a question mark. He'd have to think on it.

The Great Escape

December 14th

One a.m.

The captain, if indeed he was the captain, exited the wheelhouse. Two men trudged along behind him.

The old fisherman had been counting the men who had taken over his ship. So far, there were two Asian men who regularly came up from the hold to share a cigarette, a pilot in the wheelhouse, a short taciturn man who seemed to be the captain of the crew, and two or possibly three others. There were maybe thirty-five refugees huddled in the bowels of the hold, all families.

He had been conscious for far longer than anyone knew.

Reggie rested against the gunwale, Betty's head on his shoulder. His arms and hands were numb. Thor's hammer pounded against the inside of his skull from the whack he had received. The blanket had fallen to his waist, revealing tufts of grey hair amidst a muscled chest. Years of fishing had taught him to compartmentalize his pain and ignore the goosebumps that covered his arms and the chills that rippled through his body. He concentrated instead on *The Persephone's* speed, heading, and what chance he and Betty had to escape.

He watched the three men approach, his eyes as icy as the fog that wrapped his boat in its cold embrace, brushing against his face with a lover's gentle touch. The mist was laden with salt. He could taste it.

The Persephone's bow sliced through the water. The hollow noise the water made against the wooden hull told him that they were in deep water.

"Good, you're awake," the leader said, squatting in front of his grizzled captive. "My helmsman is having a hard time navigating this channel in the fog. You look like the man for the job. He says your navigation instruments are finicky."

"And why should I help the likes of you," Reggie fumed, inwardly pleased that the man didn't know where they were. Reggie suspected they were entering the Queen Charlotte Sound. He could sense it in the rumble the engines made in the fog and the feel of the boat beneath him.

"Manners mate," one the crewmen snapped, booting Reggie in the side.

Reggie harrumphed and glared at the man, barely moving an inch.

The smuggler lifted a foot to kick the bound man again.

"Enough," the captain ordered.

"Sorry about that," the captain continued. "My men are a little stressed. Apparently, they don't deal with that well."

"Not my problem," Reggie snorted with disdain.

"Let's be honest here, shall we? I don't think you want to drown alongside your beautiful wife, do you?"

Champ growled menacingly, not liking the smuggler's tone.

Betty opened her eyes, a pained expression on her face as she sat up. She pursed her lips, her eyes glittering in the faint glow cast by the red and white running lights.

The Border collie sidled up to the squatting man. He scratched it under the chin. The dog thumped its tail and then curled up beside Betty once again.

"Maybe a ringside seat in Davy Jones' locker doesn't scare me," Reggie rumbled. "I know it doesn't scare my wife; does it honey?"

"Not a bit," Betty said bravely.

The captain laughed.

The two men behind him snickered.

"They're full of it, boss," the taller of the crewmen said, glaring down at them.

Reggie could see the two crewmates were itching to boot him again. Hair trigger tempers. Good to know.

"No, I don't think they are," the boss whispered. "These two are something that you'll never be."

"What's that," the tall crewman barked.

Reggie chuckled.

His wife tensed but remained silent.

"They're fearless," the boss man replied.

"What's in it fer us," Reggie asked after a moment.

"I'll let you get dressed," the captain replied. "How's that for a start?"

"As you said, that's a start," Reggie agreed. "What else?"

"Don't push your luck."

"Let my dog go, he won't hurt anyone," Betty piped up.

"What she says," Reggie agreed.

"You want me to let your guard dog off that chain," the captain purred. "Let him and the two of you loose on my boat?"

"Something like that," Reggie retorted, careful not to challenge this bozo. "I figure we're entering Queen Charlotte Sound, in the dead of night, in a fog so heavy ya can't see the running lights on the bow. Unless yer pilot knows these waters like the back of his hand like I do, we'll all be sharing a pint with Davey afore long."

"Point taken," the head smuggler sighed. "Here's the deal though. The muzzle stays on. If he misbehaves, I'll toss him overboard myself. It will pain me greatly. I love dogs. You can both get changed, one at a time, and then I'm going to tie your missus up in the pilot house beside you. If you give me any trouble whatsoever, I'll have one of my men shoot her. I don't feel the same about killing people as I do about killing dogs. Are we clear on that?"

"I can live with it," Reggie hissed.

Betty twitched beside him. He knew she was amused.

Reggie nudged her.

"Sorry," she mumbled, contrite.

God, but she was a strong woman, Reggie grinned, exchanging a look with the puzzled captain. The smuggler's boss' eyebrows rose perceptibly, and a look of respect crossed his angular face.

"Cut our new pilot here loose," the captain ordered his men. "Once he's dressed and, on the bridge, release the woman. Leave the dog for last."

The two crewmen grunted. One of them roughly sliced through Reggie's bonds, obviously not happy with his boss's plans.

Reggie nodded at Betty.

She nodded back.

A plan started forming in his mind. If it meant losing *The Persephone* to save their lives, then so be it.

***

Sam dragged herself into the cottage. She was exhausted. She had gotten used to being up late waiting for her daddy to come home from work. A couple of days on Seal Island had changed all that. She was up early and in bed by ten o'clock. The stern people on the walls approved. She could feel it. Some of them watched her, especially the lady who used to own the house.

"You okay, sweetie," her father asked.

"Just tired," she replied sleepily.

"I'm sorry I yelled at you back there," Chris apologized. "I'm glad you've met some new friends."

"I know, Daddy," she mumbled, dragging the velvet bag of food across the floor.

"I'll tell you what, we'll hang that pretty Christmas ornament in the front window tomorrow after breakfast," he grinned.

"That would be awesome," Sam mumbled, trying to sound excited.

She was bone weary. Her cheeks burned now that they had left the frosty night behind them. She felt like she had lead weights on her feet.

Sam looked up at her father. He looked as tired and hollow eyed as she was. It was clear he was upset and more than a little worried. This was the third job in a row that didn't go well for her daddy.

Maybe that was the problem?

Maybe Daddy was worried they wouldn't have the best Christmas ever, even though they had an amazing turkey?

"Daddy," Sam said, brightening. "Can we cook the turkey tomorrow? We don't have to wait until Christmas, do we?"

Chris burst out laughing.

"We could, I suppose," he admitted, fingering the whiskers on his chin. "Come on, let's see how thawed out our turkey is. Hopefully, it didn't get damaged when it bounced off your friend Gertrude's head."

That caused Sam to giggle, the image of a stunned Gertrude looking bewildered after being smacked in the head by a turkey.

Father and daughter walked into the kitchen. Chris removed the turkey from his large loot bag. The turkey was the only item in the bag.

"It looks all right," he said, examining the turkey. "What do you think?"

"I think it looks scrumptious," Sam agreed. "And there is a can of cranberry sauce in the pantry. There's a box of stuffing mix and we got potatoes on your last job."

"Since when did you become such a Martha Stewart," Chris marveled.

"I watch the cooking channel when we have internet," Sam beamed, suddenly wide awake.

"Okay, tomorrow we'll cook Christmas dinner," her father agreed, placing the turkey in the kitchen sink. "We'll be back on the boat for Christmas and we can't cook that turkey in the catamaran's tiny oven."

Her daddy seemed in a much better mood now. Sam was glad. Maybe she would find something to wrap the gold coin in and gift it to him in the morning. That would make him happy.

Sam had hidden the coin inside a teddy bear she found in the closet. The teddy bear smelled sour and was missing an eye but was perfect for hiding treasure.

"Can I invite Also to dinner," Sam asked.

Her father's face turned purple. He was angrier than she'd

ever seen him, even more than when he met Gertrude.

"No, I don't want strangers in the house," he seethed, pointing a warning finger at her. "That boy is too old to be your friend. I don't want you hanging around with him anymore."

"I know he's old, but he's harmless," she sulked. "And Also's not a stranger. He's nice. You haven't hardly even met him."

"Look, Sam," her father replied, bending down on one knee to look her in the eye. "I could see enough to recognize that your friend is special. I'm sure he would never mean to harm you, but if he starts asking questions, and talks about us too much, then we're in real trouble. Get it?"

"I guess so," she whimpered, broken hearted.

Her daddy hugged her.

He was doing his best to look after her, she knew that. There was something worrying him too. She saw it in his eyes when she pulled away. Daddy was her daddy after all, and she loved him regardless of how snappy he was.

"Off to bed," he said. "I'll put everything away. Good job finding the fifty dollars too."

"Thanks, Daddy," she crooned, deciding that she wasn't quite ready to give up her treasure.

Tomorrow was another day. She hoped a good old fashioned turkey dinner would lighten her father's spirits.

***

Ida Abercrombie and Pearl Tullis sat on opposite sides of Also's double bed. Two Saint Bernard puppies and Ida's oldest breeding female, now spayed, slept on the floor at the foot of the bed, guarding the two women and the young man.

Also was bathed in sweat, his sweet face red and puffy, his wavy dark hair plastered to his head. He had been sick and feverish half the night.

"I'm not sure he's going to beat it this time, Pearl," Ida whispered over top of her sleeping nephew.

"He's a strong boy," Pearl replied, reaching across the bed to pick up one of Also's limp hands. She squeezed it lightly. The boy sighed with pleasure. "And a gift from God."

"He is a gift, my friend," Ida agreed, her face wan in the soft glow cast by the bed lamp. "I don't know what I'd do without him. This house has shined since the day he came to live with me."

The lamp on the bedstand was old, the rice paper shade yellowed and cracked with age. Ida's father had carved the stand for her when she was a little girl. It was made from a single piece of hemlock. Galloping horses pulled a stagecoach, the folk-art stylized driver yelling out commands that would never be heard... except for Also, he heard them all. There used to be a leather whip in his right hand, but the whip, the hand, and the whole right arm had broken off a long time ago.

Also loved the lamp. He said bandits chased the stagecoach and that while you couldn't see her, there was a princess inside that they were trying to kidnap to hold ransom for gold doubloons.

The story took on a life of its own from there, always changing depending on Also's imagination that day. It didn't matter that Western folklore, pirates and fantasy mixed.

Ida loved her nephew as if he were her own. He was a ray of light in a world that was sometimes far too grey. Ida's husband and son were gone, lost to the sea like so many other older widows along the coast.

Also's last round of chemo was three years ago. He almost didn't survive it. His doctor had recommended a quieter life, which is how he came to live with Ida.

"Let's wait until we know the leukemia is back," Ida comforted her. "Maybe it's just a bad case of the flu. He's been running around in the rain visiting me and hanging out with that new friend of his. They've been searching for more of the Brother's treasure. Wish folks would let the Brother rest. Nothing good ever comes from stolen money. That's what those gold coins are... people's broken dreams. Betty and Reggie were right to give the coins Gertrude dug up away."

"Who is that girl he's been hanging out with? Did you know

Charlie hired someone to look after the cottage," Ida asked, breaking out of her reverie.

"I don't know who she or her father are," Pearl answered briskly. "I called Charlie. He told me he didn't hire anyone to look after the place. He was still searching the records to find a relative. Tammy's estate's in limbo until then."

"That's interesting, isn't it," Ida frowned.

"Sam," Also gasped, his eyes fluttering open. "I gotta see Sam."

"Shhhh, everything will be all right," Ida crooned, wiping the sweat from the boy's face with a washcloth.

"No, Sam's in trouble," he croaked. "The angel told me."

Ida and Pearl glanced worriedly at each other.

"Maybe you better call the doctor, Ida," Pearl advised her friend. "He's hallucinating."

"No," Also hissed. "Sam needs me."

"How about I look in on Sam tomorrow," Pearl placated the boy. "Will that make you feel better?"

"Promise," the young man stuttered, panic stricken. "Angel says she's gotta stay away from the sorcerer."

"I promise, Also," Pearl replied earnestly.

Also nodded his head, fighting sleep.

"Knock. Knock," he murmured.

"Who's there?" Ida smiled, wiping his brow with a damp facecloth. She then placed the back of her hand on his forehead.

"You know, I think the fever is breaking," Ida said, her silvery voice as soft as a summer breeze.

Pearl sat back in her chair, sighing with relief.

"Aida," Also mumbled.

"Aida who," Ida grinned.

"Aida a sandwich for lunch," the young man finished, his head rolling sideways on the pillow.

Also began to snore.

"He got a 'knock, knock' book for his birthday and he's been hooked on knock, knock jokes ever since," Ida explained.

Pearl chortled.

The two Saint Bernard puppies stood up and wandered over

to the bed. They nosed Ida and then jumped onto the bed, sandwiching Also between them.

Mazie, the old bitch, lifted her head, drool spooling at the corners of her mouth. She fixed her eyes upon Pearl.

"Is that dog smiling at me," Pearl asked her friend, cocking her head sideways in response to the old dog's loving gaze.

"Yes, I think she is," Ida agreed. "Perhaps you should take Mazie with you in the morning. She's a good girl. I think she's chosen you. Dogs do that, you know. That's why I never sold Bessie and Bethel here. They're so bonded to Also."

"Who names your puppies," Pearl chuckled.

"Now who do you think," Ida grinned, glancing down at her nephew.

The two old women cackled like hens.

"A dog would be good company," Pearl mused aloud, "but she's too big for me to handle and what will happen if I die?"

"Mazie will look after you, dear, not the other way around," Ida informed her friend, her eyes sparkling with mischief. "That's her job. And I don't think you're going to die anytime soon. If you do, Mazie will come back to live with me. I decided to stop breeding this year. It's time for the bitches and me to retire."

Two a.m.

"*Persephone*, Alert Bay," the radio crackled, startling his wife and the boss man. "You up still, Reg?"

Reggie automatically picked up the radio, but the boss man who had been snoozing in the first mate's chair abruptly sat up.

Betty sat on the floor, bound to the chrome handle beside the hatch to the lower cabin with more plastic zip ties.

"Don't answer that," the boss man commanded.

"If'n I don't, they'll think something's wrong," Reggie replied calmly. "Up to you."

The boss man sighed.

"Okay but mind your 'p's and 'q's."

"Alert Bay, *Persephone*," Reggie drawled. "What's up? There ain't an emergency, is there?"

"Nah, RCMP called us asking about a white sailboat captained by old Saint Nick himself," came the response.

"Is he serious," the smuggler snorted.

"Some perp dressed as Santa Claus is breaking into houses on the coast," Betty informed him.

"Yeah, we heard tell of it a couple of days ago," Reggie radioed back.

"Guy's hit some more places," the Alert Bay radio operator said. "He almost got caught in Comox, and he just hit two Denman Island cottages. Homeowner swears he saw an elf with him."

Even the smuggler boss found that funny.

"Gotta hand it to the guy, he's got pizzazz," Reggie chortled.

Betty glowered at him.

Reggie grinned and shrugged.

One day maybe his wife would lighten up about that sort of thing.

"Anyways, I just wanted ta give ya a heads-up. They got a BOLO out on Santa Claus and his elves last seen sailing up the coast. Over."

"Good to know," Reggie chuckled. "*Persephone*, out."

The radio crackled twice as Alert Bay signed off.

"So, now we gotta watch for Saint Nick," the smuggler crowed.

"Appears so," Reggie agreed.

The two men, even though they were at odds, roared with laughter.

His wife's jaw clenched as she shot him an evil look.

***

"I think you better stay here for the night," Ida advised her friend. "Also appears to be out of the woods and I'm knackered."

"Me too," Pearl replied wearily.

"Come on, the bed's made up in the spare room," Ida said, standing up.

The boy in the bed slept peacefully, his two best buddies wrapped around him, paws across his chest.

Pearl smiled.

The young man was in good hands.

Pearl followed Ida to the spare room, the giant chestnut, black and white Saint Bernard padding down the hall after her.

"Oh, no, you are not sleeping with me," Pearl scolded the dog.

Ida grinned and waved to her before heading down the hall to her own bedroom.

Pearl took off her sweater and pants and laid them neatly on a chair in the corner. She climbed into bed, her aged bones snapping and popping as she fluffed up the pillow and settled down for the night.

Mazie sniffed her hand.

Pearl absently reached out and stroked the dog's head.

She was halfway to sleep when the bed springs groaned, and the massive Saint Bernard climbed onto the bottom of the bed.

"Don't think this is going to happen every night," she informed the dog as she rolled onto her side.

Four a.m.

"Come on," Reggie purred into his wife's ear.

Betty stirred and lifted her head off her husband's lap.

She glanced sideways at the smuggler in the first mate's chair. The boss man had gone below decks and left one of his men to guard them.

The smuggler had been rude until Reggie had pointed him towards the stash of booze in the cupboard behind the man's back. The pot-bellied miscreant had downed a bottle of premium scotch within a couple of minutes and was now snoring heavily, his head resting upon his chest, his rifle propped against the wall.

"Reach into my back pocket and pull out my penknife, cut these damn zip ties, and I'll cut yers," he whispered huskily.

Betty carefully pulled the folding penknife from her husband's back pocket and worked at the ties that bound his wrists to the steering wheel. Once free, she handed the knife to Reggie.

Reggie bound the wheel with the line he kept for just that purpose and freed his wife.

"What about his rifle," Betty hissed. "We need it."

Reggie shook his head.

He was right. It might wake the smuggler.

They cautiously tiptoed out of the cabin, sliding the outer door open and closed with minimal noise.

The deck was empty except for the German shepherd and the Border collie.

"This way," Reggie said, leading Betty by the arm.

"No barking, boys," she mumbled to the dogs.

Champ and the collie wagged their tails.

"What about Mugsy," Betty quaked. "I don't want to leave him."

"You heard the boss man, he wouldn't hurt a dog," Reggie assured her. "And I saw the little guy asleep on our bed when boss man went to bed."

Betty cringed, but she knew if they were going to get away, it was now or never. The smugglers were all asleep.

"Where are we going," Betty murmured.

"We're gonna steal one of the dinghy's," he replied. "I know where we are. There's an old Haida village not far from here. We'll take the dogs and hunker down there."

"Okay," Betty nodded, worried. "You're sure?"

"I'm sure," he grinned. "That pilot they got ain't very good. I think he knows he's over his head and doesn't want the boss to know it."

Betty's whole body trembled. The icy air bit through the strands of her sweater.

Reggie grabbed the wool blankets that the dogs had been sleeping on as they crept past the hold. The hatch was locked, keeping the folks below safe from the bitter north wind.

They scurried to the back of the boat.

Two rowboats bobbed on their lines in the stern's wake.

Reggie pulled one of the boat's in. The wake wasn't that large, her husband having informed the boss man that he didn't want to go too fast in the fog. The GPS was known to falter in these waters. The boss' pilot had backed him up.

Betty leapt into the boat. Both dogs followed her without being prompted. She reached out to her husband for the blankets.

Instead of handing her the blankets, Reggie grabbed a Billy bat and a fishing box and tackle from the back of the rowboat tied to the trawler's stern. He handed them to Betty.

Reggie then tossed down the blankets, sliced the line on the second skiff, and then jumped in beside Betty and the dogs. He sliced the line to their dinghy and patted the seat beside him.

Betty grinned and snuggled up beside her husband as *The Persephone* chugged away, the massive engines aiding in the couple's escape as the ship headed out to sea.

Betty placed two of the blankets on the bottom of the skiff for the dogs and shook out the last one, draping it over her knees.

"Start rowing, my love, it'll keep ya warm," her husband rumbled, his voice breaking with emotion.

The collie curled up on a blanket. Champ watched the retreating trawler until it was no longer visible in the night, its lights fading into the layers of fog.

Betty was relieved that the waves weren't any bigger than traffic bumps. The wind, though stinging, was light. The current appeared to be with them.

"That was almost too easy," she purred, rowing in unison with the man she loved more than life itself.

"That's cause those boys are thick," Reggie explained. "I don't think they're real smugglers."

"What makes you say that?" she queried, intrigued.

"First off, that pilot really has no idea what he's doing," Reggie continued. "The GPS works fine. It works off'n a satellite and I had the charts open to track where we were. That fella who was captaining the lot. He wasn't no killer. I've seen enough bad ones in my life and so have you. It's in the eyes. He didn't have killer eyes."

"I don't know, honey," Betty sighed. "We've been wrong about that before. Look at Gwen and Camille. I didn't peg those two as killers."

"I think ya would have if'n yer weren't so close to them," Reggie responded.

Nice words. She knew he was trying to make her feel better. Guilt still niggled at her. It had taken too long to solve the deaths of Summer River and Tiffany Hyde-White.

"What about your boat," she asked. "You love *The Persephone*. What will happen to her?"

"She'll be fine," he grinned. "I sent her on a course straight out ta sea. That pilot may be daft and inexperienced, but he should figure it out once one of those bozos wakes him up. I heard a fella ask the boss man when they'd get to Rupert. Folks will know something's wrong once they see *The Persephone* without me piloting her."

"I never knew you were so devious," she crooned.

"Well, ya never caught me when I was smuggling my pot, did ya," he responded.

"Did it ever occur to you that I never tried to catch you."

"Now who's the devious one," he laughed.

Betty stopped rowing and threw her arms around her husband. She kissed him.

"Aye, that's enough, young lady, ya'll tip us over," her husband replied as the boat rocked crazily from side to side.

Spirit Song

December 14th - afternoon

Sam sat in the kitchen staring at the tin foil covered turkey in the oven. She had already peeled a pot full of potatoes. They stood on the stove waiting to be cooked. She had found a couple of turnips in the garden that Gertrude had missed. They were in the sink, waiting to be peeled.

A soft snore erupted from her father snoozing in a Lazy Boy chair in front of the fireplace. He had put on an old black and white western movie. Men on horses raced across the desert on the television screen for no apparent reason other than that was what the movie people thought people did in those days.

The smell of roasting turkey filled the house with its mouth-watering savory scent.

Sam wondered where her friends were. She hadn't seen Also, Gertrude or Peaches all day and it was almost two o'clock.

She fingered the gold coin in her pocket, rubbing it between her thumb and forefinger for good luck. If she didn't have to watch the turkey cook, she would have taken her shovel and sneaked back to Brother Twelve's cabin. She was sure there were mason jars filled with gold buried beneath the bed.

If she had a lot of treasure, she'd bury it under the floorboards beneath her bed too.

Sam had dreamed about the prophet last night. He loomed over her in a flowing blue robe with golden moons and stars on it. It was a pretty robe, too pretty for a man to wear in her opinion.

Brother Twelve didn't look very happy. His breath smelled like Daddy's did after they had spaghetti and garlic bread. That had never happened before. Dreams with smell-a-vision. It would have been funny except that it wasn't.

"Mind your business," he warned her, his brown eyes narrowing in his golden-brown face. His voice was deep and commanding like her father's was when he told her to do something and he meant it.

The space behind him crackled with energy. Angry clouds gathered in her room. Lightning flashed through her bedroom.

A woman appeared behind the prophet. She was a young woman with long brown hair, red highlights and tanned skin. Sam recognized her instantly. She was in one of the pictures hanging over the fireplace in the living room.

The woman's hands were on her hips. Her gaze was so filled with malice that Sam screamed herself awake, tugging the ragged quilt she slept beneath up to her chin.

Her father raced into the room, flicking on the light and chasing the evil shadows away.

"Sweetie, what's wrong," he asked worriedly. "Did you have a nightmare?"

Sam nodded, tossed the covers aside, and threw herself into her father's arms. Tears welled in her eyes. She hated being a scaredy-cat. Big girls didn't cry.

"It was all just a bad dream," her daddy consoled her.

"I know," she squeaked. "It was so real."

"You better come with me tomorrow night," Chris said, patting her back, "maybe a night in your own bed on the *Polar Bear Express* is what you need."

"Okay," she sniffled.

The turkey in the oven hissed, startling Sam out of her reverie.

Daddy was right. She needed to spend a night in her own bed, listening to the water tap against the hull, the gentle roll of the waves rocking her to sleep.

She would miss Also when she left, but this cottage wasn't her home. It was haunted by the ghosts of people who had gone before. They weren't her people either.

The little girl sighed.

Something caught her eye, and she glanced over her shoulder.

Snowflakes fell from the sky. A large lacy one caught in the spider web at the corner of the window.

"Daddy, it's snowing," she yelled gleefully.

"Huh," her father snorted, waking abruptly.

Sam raced to the front door and threw it open.

Light grey clouds stretched across the horizon. Watchtower Mountain was shrouded in a veil of sugary candy floss. The fat snowflakes fluttered down from the sky in Nature's own ticker-tape parade. Sam wouldn't have been surprised to see a line of floats to go by.

A lone figure in a bulky blue coat and a giant dog scurried down the road, barely visible in the envelope of winter that surrounded them.

A mantle of ice ringed the person's hood. They leaned on a black cane as they pushed open the garden gate, head bent against the driving snow. The Saint Bernard followed behind.

It wasn't Crazy Morris' dog.

Who was this?

There seemed to be a lot of the friendly, furry giants on Seal Island.

Her father wandered out onto the porch and draped one arm over her shoulder as the figure approached.

"Hello," Pearl said warmly. "Isn't it beautiful?"

"It's a winter wonderland," Chris agreed.

"It's perfect. We're having our Christmas turkey today," Sam chirped. "It's the biggest turkey ever."

"How marvelous," the woman laughed.

"Do you need to come in and warm up for a minute," Chris asked, his concern for the old woman surprising Sam especially after he had just warned her about having people in.

"No, thank you, but it is nice of you to offer," the woman said, her glacial blue eyes matching the color of her coat. "I won't be staying long, not with all this snow."

"Yes, it's really coming down," Chris agreed. "I can walk you home if you like, or Sam can."

Sam thought it wonderful that her daddy was being so neigh-borly.

"That's okay, I've got Mazie to lean on if I need to," the senior chuckled.

"Is that her name," Sam asked, running out into the snow in her slippers.

The Saint Bernard snuffled the little girl's outstretched hand and nudged her. Sam staggered backwards.

"Sam," her father shouted in alarm.

Pearl steadied the girl and then put a hand in the air to stop Sam's father from coming any further. Everything was a-okay.

"You'll catch yourself a cold, just like Also if you aren't care-ful, my dear. Mind your business and your father," Pearl lightly scolded her.

"That's what the man in my dreams said to me last night," Sam gasped.

"Did he," Pearl mumbled. "What did he look like, this man in your dreams?"

"Sam, get back in the house," her daddy commanded. "The lady's right. You'll catch a cold. Look at you, you're getting covered in snow and your slippers are soaking wet."

"He had black hair and brown eyes that stared right through me," Sam answered, taking a step backwards. "And he wore a navy-blue robe with gold moons and stars and suns on it."

"Interesting," the old woman nodded, her face scrunching up as if she were thinking long and hard. "I actually came over to let you know that Also is sick, so you won't be seeing him for a few days. He's come down with a terrible flu."

"Sam!"

"Coming Daddy," she replied.

"I best be off," Pearl replied, softening, "but perhaps your daughter could walk me home? The snow is getting a little deep. Mazie can help me only so much. It wasn't snowing when I left the house."

"I don't mind, Daddy," she smiled at her father as she danced up the two stairs leading to the covered porch, turning on the charm.

"Yes, it's a good idea," he agreed, "but come home right away. I don't want you trapped by a blizzard. You don't want to miss Christmas dinner either, do you?"

"I'll come right back," Sam beamed, slipping into her rainbow-colored rubber boots and a fleece lined purple ski jacket. "And don't forget to baste the turkey, Daddy."

Chris roared with laughter, Pearl joining in.

"I won't, sweetie," he grinned.

Sam didn't understand what was so funny. Basting the turkey was an important job. Daddy was the one who told her so.

The little girl scampered down the stairs and into the yard. She led the way out of the yard.

"Take my arm," Pearl addressed the girl, her voice husky, as the two stepped onto the gravel road, "here just under the elbow. I don't need you to hold me up, it is just for balance. I don't want to use my cane. It might slip. At my age, I break easy."

Sam slipped her tiny arm beneath the older woman's and they strolled down the road like lovers, the Saint Bernard galloping off to play in the snow at the side of the road.

Several inches of snow had settled on the ground. The evergreens looked like someone had sprinkled icing powder on their leaves.

"So, young lady, tell me more about your dream," the wizened woman queried.

Sam bit her lip, not sure how much she should tell her. If she had a grandma, she would wish her to be like Pearl Tullis. Pearl made the most awesome jam and biscuits, and Sam felt all warm and fuzzy around her, but Sam wasn't sure she wanted to talk about her dream. Of course, talking about it though might help the images burned into her mind go away.

"He told me to 'mind my business'," she stuttered. "He was scary, and he smelled like garlic. I've never had a dream where I smelled stuff."

"That was definitely Brother Twelve," Pearl sighed.

"There was an angry lady with him too. She appeared during

the lightning storm. She looked like the picture above the fire-place, long brown hair and tanned skin."

"That would be my friend, Tammy Smith," Pearl gasped. "She was about your age when she met Brother Twelve. She believed in him. No matter what I said, I couldn't talk her out of his crazy preaching's. I was the only one who knew. Her parents would have sent her away if they found out, and I didn't want that. Tammy was my best friend. I guess the Brother came for her after all. I don't know why she'd be angry with you though."

"I knew there was a ghost in the house," Sam croaked.

"I need you to promise me something, young lady."

Sam put one hand behind her back and crossed her fingers. You couldn't break a promise if you did that. She read about it in a book.

"I want you to promise me that you won't go on any more treasure hunts and you will stay away from Brother Twelve's cabin," Pearl said in earnest.

"I promise," Sam agreed. "But what if Also wants to go?"

"His auntie and I have already made him promise the same thing. Also takes his promises seriously. I hope you do too."

Sam didn't have to answer because they were already in front of Pearl's cottage. It looked so pretty, the yellow siding with the white trim, and the snow mounding on the roof.

"Would you like a jar of blackberry jam to go home with," the old woman asked the girl, seeming to take Sam's silence as agreement to uphold her promise.

"Yes, thank you," Sam replied politely.

"Come on, Mazie, in we go," Pearl called the dog.

The Saint Bernard jogged out of the flurry of white, the hair on its back a blanket of ice. It looked more like the Abominable Snowman than a dog.

Pearl and Mazie went into the house while Sam waited out-side, feeling bad that she had crossed her fingers and lied to the nice lady. She opened her mouth and caught a snowflake on her tongue. It was bitterly cold.

"Here you go," Pearl said, holding out a paper bag with a jar of jam and a loaf of freshly baked bread inside.

Sam's eyes lit up.

"You can have bread and jam for dessert after your Christmas dinner," the woman grinned.

Sam hugged Pearl fiercely for no other reason than the kindness offered by the little old lady touched her heart. It had always been she and daddy against the world. This woman offered something new, and Sam didn't quite know how to react.

"I want you to know that despite your dream, Tammy will never hurt you," the old woman advised her, "and if you ever need help, you can always count on me."

Sam wasn't sure why she would ever need help from Pearl Tullis when she had her daddy, but she was glad she was now a friend of the lady who was a friend of Tammy Smith. If she ever dreamed about the lady who owned the house again, she would tell her that.

***

Betty huddled in the boat's bow, a blanket beneath her and a blanket wrapped tightly around her shoulders having 'borrowed' one of the two dog blankets. She didn't mind the smell of wet dogs and mold that permeated the material anymore, either that or the cold wet air had washed out the stink. She would have found it funny if she weren't so darned cold.

Reggie had draped the last blanket over his shoulders as he continued rowing by himself. The dogs hadn't been impressed.

Her arms ached from four hours of sitting alongside him, tugging and pushing the oar back and forth, the fingers on both her hands cramping into claws as the dinghy bounced over the water.

The Border collie lay on her feet, sound asleep. Betty felt her eyes closing too but would wake up every time her chin touched her chest.

Champ leaned against Reggie's legs, keeping a watchful eye out for signs of the smugglers who stole their boat. Betty cursed the men, but not the families huddled inside *The Persephone's* hold. She worried about them. What unimaginable pain they must be in.

What were the smugglers' plans?

Would the people be indentured or enslaved here in Canada by the smugglers?

Were they refugees from an internment camp?

Who was the man with the bible or Koran who had insisted that the smuggler give them a blanket?

The answers eluded her.

Betty thought about asking her husband if he wanted her to take over, but the last two times she had asked he had smiled and shook his head.

Snow was falling. It started twenty minutes ago. It was light at first, but now she could barely see the hauntingly beautiful forest that lined the shore.

"I think this is it," Reggie boomed, his head and shoulders covered in a dusting of snow.

"I hope so, we need shelter, honey," Betty stuttered, her teeth chattering. "It's getting worse."

"Aye, I know. The place I'm looking fer should be around the point," he said, nodding towards a rocky knoll with frothy waves slapping against it.

The seaman grunted and hauled on the oars, the dinghy plunging into the surf as it rounded the rocky jetty.

Through the snowy haze, Betty could see a couple of ancient totem poles pointing at the sky. A bear was atop of one pole, a salmon at his feet, and a raven topped another, its wings raised as if it was ready to take flight. Several more totem poles lay on the forest floor, time toppling all but the hardiest of them.

"We're here," Reggie grinned. "Back in the trees is a long house. It's busted up, but the main section is still standing. At least, the last time I was here, it was."

White snow. Silver totems. Moss covered giant evergreens towering above a grey ocean. Whispers of an ancient race.

The spirit of the totems and the long house only now visible in the trees as they beached the dingy brought tears to her eyes, the experience so mystical that it left Betty speechless.

The dogs jumped out of the boat and raced happily across the beach and into the trees.

"Let them go," Reggie muttered, as if reading her thoughts.

She didn't want the dogs to disturb anything, not here, not in this sacred place.

"If'n there're any critters around, they'll smell the dogs and take off," he assured her, pulling the rowboat higher up onto the shore with his wife still in it.

"What kind of critters," she asked meekly.

"Bears, cougars, racoons mostly," he replied, offering her his hand. "I'm hoping the long house ain't too full of scat. We need ta get us a fire going."

Betty allowed Reggie to lift her up. She was so cold that her legs buckled beneath her when she exited the boat. Reggie swept her into his arms and carried her across the beach to the tree line. He put her down and went back to retrieve the blankets, wooden club, and tackle box.

"Come on, let's get ya warm," he whispered in her ear as he passed her by.

Betty stood for a moment, regaining her land legs, and then followed the tall fisherman into the trees.

It was so beautiful, the snow falling on cedars, the flakes fat and heavy. In another place, another time, she would have happily spent hours snapping pictures and journaling about her experience. She hoped to do that more, maybe write a book about their journeys.

The long house was constructed of huge cedar logs. The totems guarding the entrance had toppled to the ground and lay there decaying beneath layers of moss. A stone fireplace with flattened stone benches took on one wall of the bleak enclosure.

Reggie stopped before the gaping entrance and mumbled something.

"What's that, honey," she asked him.

"I was just saying a prayer, asking the spirits to welcome and protect us from the storm," he muttered, his cheeks reddening.

"It's only right."

Betty smiled, her heart swelling, a warm gush spiraling outward from her chest to her fingers and toes. She felt it then, a brush of fingers on her own, a faint wisp of wind on her face, the whisper of welcome.

"Yes, it is only right," she agreed.

The two dogs came barreling out of the woods, tongues lolling, eyes bright and alive.

Betty laughed at their silly antics as they chased each other around and around the totem poles.

Reggie strode forward. He gathered up the dry mosses and branches that littered the earthen floor.

"Ya asked me how I knew those smugglers weren't the real thing," he chortled, dropping an arm full of kindling on the stone fireplace hearth.

"Hmmm," she mused, sitting down on a rock close by.

"They never checked my pockets," he laughed, pulling a Bic lighter from his front pocket. "I mean, cremini, they left me with a lighter and a pen knife."

"Small miracles, honey," she shrugged, her eyes crinkling with mirth. "Small miracles."

It didn't take long for her man to have a good fire going. He found a backpack in his travels. It was weathered and stained. A day tripper must have left it behind. The pack contained some plastic cutlery, a tin mug, plus a couple packages of instant vegetable soup.

"Seems like the spirits granted our prayers, babe," Reggie grinned. "I don't know how old this soup is, but beggars can't be choosers, as my ma used to say."

"That dehydrated stuff will outlast us," Betty mused, staring into the flames. She wrapped a blanket tightly around her shoulders.

"They're having a grand old time," he added, watching the shepherd and collie cavort.

"Without question," Betty agreed. "You must admit, we are having an exciting honeymoon. Are you sure you didn't plan all this? You know, make me love you even more."

Reggie roared with laughter, his grey eyes as deep and mysterious as the fog bank they had traversed, his steely hair a riotous mound of curls about his rugged face.

She felt guilty watching her husband do all the work. He stomped out into the snow, disappearing in a swirling white cloud, and returning with some larger sections of broken branches to keep the fire going. He then melted snow in the tin cup and dumped half of the soup mixture in, handing the cup to her once the soup had boiled.

It was the best dehydrated soup she had ever tasted. It warmed her to the core.

She knew there was no point arguing with her husband on who ate first. Her man was like that. She was becoming accustomed to it, but she would only go so far.

"Sit down," she ordered him at last, "you're wearing me out. You need fluids and a hot meal too."

"It's gonna be dark soon and I need ta make sure we got enough wood fer tonight," he growled. "It's gonna get colder. We might be here fer a couple of days by the look of it."

"Sit. Down. Eat," Betty commanded.

"I didn't know'd I'd married such a demanding woman," Reggie teased, sitting down on the flat rock beside her.

Betty stood up. Reggie reached out to stop her, but she shook off his hand, giving him an 'do you really think you're going to stop me' look.

While her husband was sipping his soup, she walked out into the storm and brought back an armload of cedar boughs. She laid them out on the floor beside the fire, placed a blanket over the boughs and then rolled the second blanket into a pillow for the two of them. By the time the bed was finished, the daylight had faded.

The dogs settled down by the fire, tired, wet and happy. They watched with interest as Reggie automatically filled the empty cup with snow and poured a smidgeon of vegetable soup on top of it before placing the tin cup on a rock by the fire to warm. They licked their lips, knowing that they would not be forgotten.

Outside, the snow sighed as it fell upon the trees in the forest, the rocks along the beach, and gathered on the seats of the rowboat. The world narrowed until nothing remained but winter white, the glow of a fire reflecting upon the silver logs of an ancient home where songs were sung and people lived, died and were born, a place where two humans, a man and a woman, nestled beneath a dirty blanket, content in their togetherness, two dogs curled up beside them, basking in the safety of what once was.

Call to Arms

December 14th - evening

"Spill the wine, dig that girl," Mac the Black of the Caribbean sang from inside his newly acquired bird cage that took up one whole side of the bar.

"Name that tune," the dreadlocked woman dressed in a flowing sage green hemp sweater and colorful hand-died floor length skirt hollered into the microphone, "for a chance to spin the wheel."

Mac-Wednesday's had become the busiest night at the pub. Not even the foot and a half of snow on the ground outside stopped people from boating in or leaving their homes for a sing along with the parrot.

On the far side of the gilded parrot cage stood a wooden spinning wheel with various pie shaped paper prizes attached to it including: win a pint, win a jug, free hat, free t-shirt, free fries, kiss the bartender, get kissed by the bartender, and dinner for two.

"April Wine," someone shouted in the back.

"Incorrect," Rainbow, the voluntary MC, laughed. Rainbow had died her dreadlocks soft shades of red, yellow, green and purple, for fun, enjoying her newfound fame.

"*Spill the Wine* by Eric Burden and War," Morris said from his bar stool, raising his glass. "Give me something harder."

"That is correct," Rainbow sashayed over to him. "Time to spin the wheel."

"I ain't spinning no wheel, Stew's on the bar," Morris stuttered.

"Ya play the game, ya spin the wheel and take yer chances,"

Rainbow grinned, mimicking the goat farmer's speech.

"Morris. Morris," the crowd chanted.

"Morris. Morris," Rainbow yelled, whipping the crowd into a frenzy.

"I told ya that ya'd rue the day ya decided ta keep that parrot and hire Rainbow here ta fix him," Morris growled at Stew, pushing his empty glass across the bar top.

"Shall I wait to see if you win a free pint first, Morris," Stew chuckled.

Morris glared at the pub owner and stood up. He hitched up his jeans as he strolled over to the spinning wheel.

"What shall it be, Morris, a pint, a jug, or maybe a kiss from Stew," the colorful pet psychic asked delightedly.

Morris grimaced, took hold of the wheel and spun it hard, hoping to break it. The red stopper ticked loudly as the wheel spun until finally coming to a stop on 'free hat'.

"Saved by destiny," Rainbow announced, reaching behind the counter and pulling out a black ball cap with a picture of a pig sewn onto it, the closest thing they could find to a bristling boar.

"Well, I could use a new hat," Morris said, waving the ball cap in the air.

A hearty round of laughter followed suit.

"Roll me over in the clover," the parrot chimed.

Leave it to Stew to find a way to make money off a cheeky mouthed parrot, Morris thought as he sat down and motioned for another beer.

"And it's no nay never," the parrot called.

"Right up your kilt," the patrons of the pub shouted over the bird's song. "No nay never no more, will I play the wild rover, no never no more."

A flurry of snow blew into the pub through the open door as Archie hustled in wearing a toque and ski jacket. He blew on his hands and walked directly up to Rainbow.

His face was grim, his eyes sunken, his back bent. For the first time, Morris thought Archie Bruce looked his age.

"Rainbow, can I borrow your microphone," he asked her.

"What's up, Archie," she queried, immediately handing him the mic.

"I can't reach my daughter," he stammered. "There's something wrong, I can feel it."

"Just flip up the black button on the side," Rainbow advised him.

"Hello, everyone," Archie's voice boomed over the speaker on a stand behind him. "I'm sorry to interrupt everyone's fun, but I can't reach my daughter. Reg isn't answering his cell phone or his radio either."

"They are on their honeymoon, Arch," a man called out.

A round of giggles and back slapping ensued.

"You don't understand," he yelled, red faced. "*The Persephone* has been spotted outside of Prince Rupert. The *Coastal Salish* captain said he passed them close enough to see that Reggie wasn't on the bridge. He didn't answer a radio call either and he tried several times."

Silence followed.

"What da ya need," a gruff fisherman growled, standing up. "We're on it."

"I need you all to get on your cell phones and call everybody you know, especially anybody who is on the water somewhere around Prince Rupert," the old man stammered. "I've called the RCMP and they're looking into it."

"They're out chasing Robin Hood," a woman smirked.

"Not Robin Hood, Santa Claus," her companion corrected her.

"They're doing their best," Archie replied, the hand holding the microphone shaking perceptibly. "Betty's one of their own. They already talked to the marina manager in Alert Bay. He spoke to Reggie late last night which is why this is so odd. If they picked anyone up, they'd have notified the Coast Guard at least. What with the weather turning, I'm afraid something's happened to them!"

"Aye and Phoenix would never let anyone helm *The Persephone*," a silver-haired old man said. "I know. I worked for him and his dad."

"Oh and talk in code or something on the radio because we don't want to let whoever is on *The Persephone* know we're onto them," Archie added.

Chairs were pushed back. Money thrown on the table. There was a mass exodus, many of the pub's patrons nodding to Archie that they were indeed 'on it' as they marched out the door.

The snow was falling ever harder outside, but it didn't deter any one of the hardy fishermen from heading to their boats.

"What can I do," Morris asked his friend.

First that fella and his daughter moving into Tammy Smith's house unannounced, the young lad falling sick, Gertrude and Peaches running haphazardly around the island at all hours of the day and night, and now this.

Morris felt his heart sink.

"Maybe you can help Rainbow with Gertrude and Peaches, Morris," Archie croaked, his voice breaking as he handed Rainbow back the microphone. "I dunno where they're at again. I don't seem to be able to keep up anymore. The past couple of years have knocked the stuffing out of me."

"We got that covered," Rainbow comforted him, with a sideways glance at Morris. "They're in our barn, safe and sound. Morris brought them over."

What was that look Rainbow just gave him all about? Did she think Archie was losing it? Did she think he didn't call Archie the next day and tell him where the animals were?

Morris had called Archie the next morning, he was sure of it. Maybe his memory was going a bit wonky too?

Archie nodded absently, his hands trembling even harder.

"How about I take ya home, Arch, and wait with ya for a while," Morris replied, truly worried for Betty's father. This wasn't like him at all.

"Thanks, Morris," Archie agreed. "Vi is pretty shaken up, but she's staying by the phone. I'd appreciate the company. Truth be told, I'm out of sorts myself. I have this feeling I can't shake that my daughter is in trouble, big time."

Morris downed his beer.

Stew waved him away when he tried to pay.

"Look after Archie," Stew mumbled. "I'm gonna make some calls too."

"Ya know, Arch, I'll call my sister. She'll get her boyfriend on it. I don't like that detective much, but he's a good copper."

"I'd appreciate that, Morris," Archie replied. "They got off to a rocky start, but Ben and Betty are friends now. He'll want to know."

"We'll find them, Archie," Stew shouted as the two men made their way to the door.

Archie nodded and tucked his head down against the icy winter blast that pelted against him as he and Morris pushed their way outside into the storm.

"And it's no nay never," the African grey parrot sang again, but this time, nobody answered.

***

Reggie wrapped himself around his wife. He could tell she was chilled to the bone. Betty wasn't as hot-blooded as he was. She was a trooper and never complained.

The Border collie stretched out under the blanket at his back snuffled, its legs moving as it dreamed. The German shepherd snuggled with Betty.

Reggie reached over his head and grabbed a chunk of wood and tossed it on the fire. Sparks flew upwards towards the high ceiling.

The fire was all that kept them from freezing to death.

Hunger gnawed at his belly.

He had tried fishing off the beach, but the fish had gone deep because of the cold. It had been too dangerous to take the boat out or to try to leave the longhouse.

Damn the snow, he cursed.

It wasn't just hampering their chances of rowing along the inlet towards Bella Coola and flagging someone down, it would drive most boat captains into harbor and make an air search impossible.

The Persephone should be in Prince Rupert unless the bozo pilot grounded her. That was a distinct possibility, too.

Betty sighed in her sleep and rolled over to face him.

Her face was flushed from being outside, her silver and blond hair falling alluringly over her face. She looked peaceful despite their predicament.

What a woman. He smiled, taking her hand in his.

He closed his eyes and rested. If the weather let up, he would try fishing again tomorrow.

In the meantime, they were safe.

At another time, maybe they would come back and stay here again.

***

Sam stared at the winter wonderland outside the kitchen window. It was so pretty she thought her heart would burst from sheer joy. Mother Nature had smiled upon them, giving her and Daddy an early Christmas after all.

Daddy was asleep in front of the fire again. Even he thought it was too dangerous to go to work tonight.

That was perfect.

Sam turned back to her chores. She put tinfoil and plastic wrap over the turkey. It seemed like they had hardly made a dent in it. Thankfully, the cooked turkey seemed to weigh less than it did frozen, and she could squish it into the fridge without help.

There weren't any mashed potatoes left, but there was a ton of gravy. Tomorrow, Daddy said, they would go to the store and actually buy some bread.

Sam didn't remember the last time they had gone grocery shopping.

Since he was in such a good mood, she asked Daddy if she could drop a turkey leg off to Also's auntie to make him some turkey soup. Daddy always made chicken soup for her when she was sick, but turkey soup would be even better, Sam thought.

Sam was surprised when her father had agreed.

She had already busted a leg off and wrapped it up ready for delivery. It was on the top shelf in the refrigerator, so every time she opened the fridge, she would see it.

That's what friends were for. They looked out for each other. Family did too. Go ahead, open any book, be it *The Polar Bear Express* or any of the Narnia books, and Nancy Drew too. She had never heard of Nancy Drew until they came to live here. Tammy Smith had all the Nancy Drew books stacked on a bookshelf in the bedroom where Sam slept. Sam had already devoured three of them, enjoying the sassy girl detective's solving of the mysteries in the stories.

Since Sam had talked to Mrs Tullis, the house felt more welcoming. She was relieved. Sam didn't want to have any more nightmares.

There was a crash at the back door.

Sam gasped.

"Daddy," she croaked, frightened.

Her daddy continued to snore, unaffected by the series of bumps in the night.

Sam crept to the back door. She wouldn't unlock it. That would be stupid. There was a peephole in it though, and it wouldn't hurt to see what was out there. If a monster was at the door, she would scream. Daddy wouldn't be snoring anymore after that; he would protect her. He always did.

The little girl inched forwards.

She heard whining. Claws scraped against the back door. The scratching was followed by another hollow thump.

Sam stood on her tippy toes and peeked through the peephole, bracing herself in case there really was a purple people eating monster at the door. Instead of screaming at the top of her lungs, she broke into a series of giggles and flung the door wide.

A furry snow-covered beast sat there looking pleased with itself. Its back was covered with snow and icicles hung from the hair on its legs and belly. The dog charged past her and into the house.

"Hey," she crowed. "Stop, you'll wake Daddy."

The dog whipped around, spit flying, tail wagging.

It was Crazy Morris' Saint Bernard.

Sam was about to close the door when a black and white bullet shot through it. Max, the Border collie, was as ice ringed and snow covered as his brother.

"What are you guys doing here," she whispered to the dogs.

The Border collie slunk under the kitchen table and laid down, trying to be as inconspicuous as possible.

"Did Crazy Morris leave you out in this storm," the girl asked the dogs.

The collie whimpered and lowered its head.

The Saint Bernard pushed its cold snout into her face.

"I bet you haven't eaten yet either, have you," she giggled, hugging the wet dog. "Good thing we have lots of turkey. There are a couple spoonsful of mashed potatoes left too since I haven't scrubbed the pot yet."

Sam pulled the turkey out of the fridge and placed it on the counter. The Saint Bernard looked at her expectantly.

The snippet of a girl washed out the bowl they had used to serve the mashed potatoes in and the smaller bowl they had put the can of corn in and diced up some leftover turkey. She then scraped the potato bits on top of the turkey and added a dollop of gravy to each.

The Border collie sidled out from under the table and lay beside its giant friend in the middle of the kitchen. Water pooled beneath the two dogs as the snow melted from their coats.

Sam deposited the bowls in front of the dogs with an award-winning smile.

"Wow, you guys were hungry," she mumbled, the turkey and gravy gone in seconds.

Sam put the turkey away and placed the empty bowls in the sink to soak.

"Okay," she whispered, "I'm not putting you guys back outside, but you have to be quiet, you hear? You'll have to go in the morning before Daddy gets up."

Sam walked over to the back door to grab a mop and bucket. She mopped up the floor as best she could.

"Come on you two," she waved to the dogs. "You can sleep in my room."

Sam crept down the hall, the two dogs following obediently behind her. If her daddy found them, she would be in so much trouble, but a heart wanted what a heart wanted, and the frozen dogs were staying with her tonight.

Sam closed the bedroom door behind the dogs. The Border collie hopped onto the bed. The Saint Bernard laid down on the round rag rug on the floor.

Sam changed into her pjs and climbed into bed. The collie snuggled up beside her.

"You guys will protect me from bad dreams, won't you," she smiled and turned off the lights.

***

Chris woke to the sound of the eleven o'clock news on the radio talking about a weather event sweeping down from the north.

He glanced out the window.

It was a weather event alright.

He yawned and stretched. The snowstorm was hampering his plans, but he had to admit it was nice to be inside this cozy little cottage instead of on the catamaran.

He stood up and wandered into the kitchen.

Sam had put away the food and washed most of the dishes. There were a couple of pots soaking in the sink. He smiled. She was a good kid.

Chris let the water go and rinsed off the two remaining items.

He wandered down the hall and into the bathroom. After a quick face wash and a brush of his teeth, he ambled out of the bathroom and went to check on his daughter.

He opened his daughter's bedroom door and stopped short.

Sam was surrounded by fur. Her face was barely visible between the giant mass of black, brown, and white. The two dogs looked up at him through sleepy eyes.

The collie nestled closer to his daughter, as if that were possible.

The Saint Bernard thumped its tail against the wall. It sounded like a kettledrum.

Chris could have sworn the dog was grinning.

He slowly closed the door. He should be furious. Chris lowered his head and chuckled. The chuckle turned into a hearty laugh.

Chris had no idea where the mutts had come from and decided he didn't want to know. His daughter was happy. They had a wonderful day. Why spoil it now?

As Chris walked back to his bedroom, he realized that it was time to settle down. They had been living on the boat for six years. Sam couldn't live that way forever. The broken look she had given him when he told her he didn't want her to hang out with that special boy haunted him.

Who was he to deny her friends?

He had done his best.

Maybe he'd try to find the real lawyer for the estate, not the one he had made up. Maybe he had enough stuffed away in the safe deposit box in Vancouver, coupled with the money he had tucked away on the boat over the last two months, to buy this cottage.

The cottage was dated, and a bit run down, but he and Sam could paint it, fix it up.

Maybe, he rationalized, maybe.

Maybe this was his call to arms to be a better father.

Pursuit

December 15th – morning

"The boats that didn't leave last night are heading out this morning now that the snow has let up," Morris informed Pearl over tea.

"Let's pray that we are back to rain by this afternoon," Pearl trembled. "I've been up most of the night worrying about them. One of the ladies from the Writer's Society was at the pub when Archie made his announcement and called me. I am so glad you stopped in to update me, Morris."

Pearl's eyes were red rimmed.

Morris could see she'd been crying.

"Ya know," he said, changing the subject. "The funniest thing happened ta me today."

"Oh," the old woman said, raising her eyes to look steadily into his.

"My dogs didn't spend the night with you, did they," Morris inquired politely.

"No, why do you ask?"

"In all the hubbub last night, I forgot ta put them in," he shrugged. "I didn't mean ta be gone all night, but I was afraid to leave Archie and the judge by themselves. They were in a state, let me tell ya, didn't settle down until Alana called me back and said that her boyfriend and his partner put the RCMP on high alert. The RCMP sent out two Coast Guard hovercrafts and the RCMP cutter stationed out of Vancouver."

"That is marvelous news," Pearl agreed, and then took a long sip of tea.

"When I got home this morning," Morris continued, "the boys

were waiting fer me and they were dry as a bone. They could have slept in the barn with the goats, but they didn't smell like goats so that seemed unlikely. They weren't even interested in breakfast. That just ain't like Brutus. The big fella can eat."

"That is odd, Morris. Where do you think they could have gone? Have you checked with Ida?"

"Called her first thing. She said 'nope'. She hadn't seen them."

Morris and Pearl drank their tea.

Morris noticed a tray of sliced turkey on the kitchen counter. It was wrapped in cellophane and had a purple bow on it, the kind you put on a Christmas present.

"That was a gift from Sam," Pearl grinned noticing Morris' questioning look.

"The little girl that lives with her pa at Tammy's," he stammered.

"Yes. She dropped it off a little while ago on her way to see Also," Pearl smiled. "She's a lovely thing. Her father popped down with her and shoveled the walkway for me."

"I still think those two are fishy," Morris muttered. "I'm keeping an eye on them like I told ya I would."

"Hmmm, I was worried at first too, Morris, but now I'm not so sure," Pearl nodded. "They're nice. I hope they stay a little longer. I'd like to find out more about them. Frankly, I think they are in trouble and I want to help. Something tells me they could use a helping hand."

Pearl may think that, but Morris didn't agree. He kept his opinion to himself. You got to watch these old ladies on this island. They're like suffragettes trying to get the right to vote. They get a bee in their bonnet and the men are done for.

"Did her papa leave with her," Morris inquired casually.

"No, he went home," Pearl answered. "I don't think he was too fond of facing Ida's dogs. Poor fellow was terrified of Mazie."

Morris chuckled. He didn't pop round to Ida's often either even though Brutus was one of her lot.

"Where is Mazie anyways? Ida told me you took her on loan," he grinned.

Pearl wagged a finger at him across the table.

"More tea?"

"No thank-you, Pearl, I gotta git going," Morris replied, standing up.

"You may see Mazie on your way home," Pearl remarked dryly. "She's taken a shine to Sam and went with her. The way I figure it, if the snow keeps up, Sam can ride her home."

Morris and Pearl laughed heartily.

He bid the old widow adieu and was on his way. He planned on taking up residence in the prophet's cabin tonight for a while once the snow let up, or maybe sneak out to that catamaran in the McDonald's bay to snoop around.

***

"Now don't you be hugging him or anything," Ida warned Sam as she ushered Sam and Mazie into Also's bedroom. "He still might be contagious, and your daddy won't be happy with me."

"Yessum," Sam agreed.

Sam was startled by how pale her friend looked. His delicate hands were wrapped around a black and white stuffed panda bear. His eyes opened when the giant Saint Bernard stuffed her slobbery jowls in his face.

"Mazie," his voice warbled.

"Hey, Also," Sam whispered, sitting down on the chair pulled up beside his bed.

"Knock. Knock," Also croaked.

"Who's there," Sam giggled.

"Hawaii."

"Hawaii who?" Sam responded.

"Hawaii you asking me so many questions," Also laughed, bursting into a series of rib rattling hoarse coughs.

Sam instantly handed the sick teen a glass of water.

Also drank down most of the glass.

"I won't stay long," Sam said. "I brought you a turkey leg so your auntie can make you some turkey soup."

"I like turkey," Also sighed, half-closing his eyes.

The Saint Bernard nudged his hand, but Also barely had the strength to rub behind her ears. The dog stared at Also for a minute and then gave Sam a beseeching look, the old dog's rheumy eyes echoing Sam's own fears.

"Daddy and I are going out on the boat for a couple of days, but I'll come see you when we get back," she whispered.

Also didn't answer, having fallen back into a feverish sleep.

"The fever comes and goes," Ida said from behind her, startling Sam.

"Is he going to be okay," Sam asked, standing up.

"Also has had a tough time in life, Sam," Ida replied thoughtfully. "He's on antibiotics. Someone picked them up for us this morning and brought them right over. It'll take a couple of days for them to kick in."

"Oh," the young girl stammered.

She hated it when grown-ups lied to her. Ida wasn't being honest. The thought of losing her best friend made her feel sick inside.

"Is there anything I can do," she begged, hoping for an answer.

"You've already done it, sweetie," Ida breathed. "You came to visit, and you brought a nice big turkey leg to throw in the soup pot. I'm already boiling it down now."

"Come on, Mazie," Sam mumbled, patting her thigh. "I'll take you home."

The dog laid down beside the bed and rested her head on her paws.

"Don't worry about Mazie," Ida whispered into Sam's ear as she wrapped an arm around her shoulder. "She'll stay by his side until she's ready to go back to Pearl's. I'll let Pearl know. Mazie dotes on Also."

Sam's legs wobbled as she walked down the narrow hall to the door, so worried for Also that her legs felt weak. She was glad Also had his Auntie Ida and Mazie looking after him, but there had to be something she could do, something that she could give her friend to help him get better. She'd think on it while she was out with her father. Maybe they'd find the answer on one of his jobs.

That was it.

She bet someone had something other than drugs in their house that would cure her friend. Maybe she'd find a book with a miracle cure in it.

***

Reggie trudged through the snow, combing the beach. He found a sheet of plastic and a half dozen plastic water bottles. The garbage and debris folks tossed off their boats and refuse from the cruise ships heading back and forth to Alaska was a crime in his opinion. Right now, though, he wouldn't complain.

He shook the snow off the blue plastic tarp and headed back to the dinghy. With some effort, he tipped the skiff upside down. The snow sloughed off the seats and tumbled out of the bottom. He righted the little boat and tugged the tarp over top to keep it dry.

Satisfied with his work, he stopped and looked out to sea.

The Queen Charlotte Strait was mellow, the still water as grey as the clouds that hovered over it. The snow wasn't as heavy anymore. It looked like it was raining on the horizon.

That made his decision easy.

It was time to leave.

Reggie marched back up his trail to camp, his footprints widening as the snow melted.

"Bets, I got us some bottles to pack drinking water," he said as he strode into camp.

Smoke from the fire rose upwards. It caught in the eve of the longhouse, and then drifted along the roofline, before it escaped into the leaden sky.

"Does that mean we're pulling up stakes," she grinned, her blue eyes calmly regarding him.

"It does," he agreed, dropping the plastic bottles by the fire. "We'll boil some snow and fill these here bottles with it. We might not have any food, but at least we won't be thirsty."

His wife nodded and pulled the tin cup off the fire. She

swished the boiling water around in each of the bottles to steril-ize them and poured it out. The two dogs watched her from their bed on the cedar boughs beside the crackling fire.

"Come on, move you two," Reggie ordered the shepherd and collie. "We're gonna put these cedar boughs on the bottom of the boat so ya won't freeze yer bums."

Betty chuckled. Her stomach growled in protest.

"Sorry," she blushed.

"Ah, don't be sorry luv, I'm starving too," he whispered husk-ily.

Betty nodded and re-filled the tin cup with ice and snow. As it melted, she kept filling it until it was full.

Reggie scooted the dogs from their bed, folded the ragged wool blankets into a rectangle, and then rolled them into a tight ball. He then dragged the cedar boughs down to the boat.

Hail sized pellets smattered against the ground, tinging as they hit the exposed sections of the aluminum dinghy, and stinging his face. His hands were stiff, the skin red and irritated.

If they were going to go, it needed to be soon.

He thought he saw a boat cruise by in the distance, but he wasn't sure. It was grey against grey. The visibility was poor. Still, it heartened him.

Perhaps the news was out.

Perhaps someone had discovered the stolen trawler.

He could only hope.

Reggie returned to camp, grabbed the rest of the boughs off the barren ground and hauled them to the shore. When he re-turned, Betty was ready. The bottles didn't have caps, so she only filled them halfway.

"Let's kick some snow over the fire," he suggested.

Betty nodded and shoveled armfuls of snow into the long-house. Reggie kicked it over the fire. The flames sputtered and steamed.

Once the remaining logs were cool enough, he dragged them outside and rolled them in the snow until they were out.

The dogs thought it was marvelous fun and buried their faces in the snow, their snouts coming out ringed with ice.

"It looks like the weather is turning," Betty mused aloud, looking up at the leaden sky.

"You know what they say," Reggie joked.

"Wait ten minutes and it'll change," she grinned.

Satisfied that the fire was out, Reggie, Betty, and the dogs slip-slided their way down the trail that Reggie had worn in the now receding snowdrifts towards the water.

Reggie tugged off the tarp and handed it to Betty to cover herself and their small amount of gear. He pushed the dingy into the water.

"In ya go, everyone," he told them.

The dogs jumped into the middle of the boat and settled down quickly on the cedar boughs. Betty stepped gingerly around them and sat down in the bow. She tucked the blue tarp around her and waited for Reggie to push the boat into the water before he sat down and picked up the oars.

"Not yet, buster," she chimed, handing her husband a blanket. "Wrap this around your shoulders. I've got the tarp so I'm good."

"Always with the orders," he chuckled and accepted the blanket.

Reggie tossed it over one shoulder, wearing the green and black wool blanket like a tartan.

"That's not good enough," she warned him, handing him a second blanket.

He grinned as he laid that blanket over his legs, folding the bottom over the two dog's rumps as the rowboat drifted out to sea on the current.

He tugged his sweater sleeves over his hands, picked up the oars, and started rowing as the hail turned to a wet sleet. It was cold. Reggie could see his breath. It wasn't so cold as to make it unbearable, at least, not in his mind.

"I thought I saw a boat in the fog earlier," he said. "I figured I'd row out into the strait for a bit and then turn level to the land. Our best chance for getting picked up is to head up the inlet to Bella Coola. It ain't that far."

Betty nodded. She huddled in the bow, wearing the tarp like a raincoat. His wife was a robust woman. Her lips rose at the sides in a thin-lipped smile. Her cheeks were flushed. Sleet dampened her nose. She searched the horizon while he put his back into it and rowed with the current, the dinghy skimming over the water.

Reggie wondered about that look, and then he realized something. His wife, though cold and hungry, was having the time of her life.

**

Benny Lee and his crew left the harbor in Bella Coola as soon as the sleet turned to rain. He had three extra crewmen on board, all of them part of the local Search and Rescue organization. They had brought extra binoculars, an infrared scanner, and various types of rescue lines.

Despite his sneaky escapade with the parrot, a fellow seaman and his wife were in trouble. His seiner would not stay in port.

News travelled fast among the west coast fishing fleets. The Coast Guard and RCMP cruisers were steaming towards Prince Rupert in pursuit of *The Persephone*. Whoever had taken the trawler were in for a barrel of trouble, especially if a fellow fisherman got there first.

Benny led a flotilla of boats. There were at least seven seiners and trawlers behind him followed by at least ten Native boats in all shapes and sizes as well as six pleasure craft.

Two of his crew and one of the Search and Rescue team were on deck, scanning the coastline. The other three men shared the bridge with him, their eyes searching the water for signs of bodies. God forbid it would come to that.

When they hit the open water, the flotilla spread out, the larger boats heading out to sea, the smaller boats staying close to the shoreline.

Benny had tuned his radio to the RCMP and Coast Guard channel as had everyone else in the newly christened 'Fishermen's Posse'.

"*Persephone*, this is the *Atlin Post*," the radio blared. "Cut your engines."

Everyone on the bridge snapped to attention.

"*Persephone*, respond. Over," the Coast Guard captain the stolen boat's bridge crew.

"*Persephone*, this is the RCMP vessel, *Nadon*," the radio crackled again. "Cut your engines. This is your final warning. Prepare to be boarded."

Benny and his crew held their breath, waiting for the response.

"*Nadon, Atlin Post, Coastal Salish* ready to assist," the captain of the *Coastal Salish* kicked in.

"*Nadon, Atlin Post, Sea Dog* ready to assist."

"*Nadon, Atlin Post, Gone Fishing* ready to assist," the radio crackled again.

"Lordie, how many of them are there," one of Benny's crewmen hissed as ten more of the Fishermen's Posse radioed in offers to help.

The air in the cabin was tense. Benny glanced around at his crew; he wasn't the only one holding his breath.

"*Nadon, Atlin Post, Persephone* cutting engines," came the terse reply.

"That weren't Reggie," Benny growled.

Benny and his first mate held eye contact.

"Right, everyone, Reggie and his wife are out there somewhere, let's find them," his first mate told the others.

The men nodded solemnly.

"Let the men outside know what's happened," Benny ordered his men.

His first mate opened the door and shouted out the situation to the men on deck. They raised a hand, showing that they'd heard and returned to their search.

The men on the bridge would relieve them in thirty minutes, every one of them aware that hypothermia was a killer, especially in this weather.

"*Sea Dog*, you see this," the radio blared.

"What's going on," one of the Search and Rescue team asked.

"Shhh," Benny ordered him.

"Yeah, there must be three dozen Chinese folks coming out of that hold," the *Sea Dog* responded.

"Half of them are women and children," the *Gone Fishing* captain responded.

"By jeez, looks like traffickers," *Sea Dog* spat into the radio.

Benny fumed, his chest constricting, knowing the hell these people had endured. He had been smuggled into Canada illegally when he was a boy. His sister died of pneumonia on the way here because of the deplorable conditions on the boat. The smugglers had tossed her body overboard as if she was rubbish.

"*Nadon, Atlin Post, Coastal Salish*. That's a lot of folks," the *Coastal Salish* responded. "If you need help transporting, we've got room."

"*Coastal Salish, Nadon*. We've got another boat coming," replied the captain of the *Nadon*. "Thanks for the offer. Over."

"Right, we are gonna head south once we get out of the inlet," Benny boomed. "Let's focus on our own rescue mission now."

There was silence once again in the wheelhouse as everyone returned to their posts.

Hallelujah

December 15th – late afternoon

Betty refused to allow her husband to continue.

His face was lined with exhaustion, fingertips white, lips blistering.

The dogs shivered at the bottom of the boat, their coats soaking wet, their ears flattened against their heads, their bellies laying in at least four inches of rainwater.

"Stay within sight of land," Reggie drawled, tugging the blue tarp over his shoulders.

Betty settled herself down, pulled the wet wool blanket over her shoulders, and wrapped the other blankets over the shivering dogs. Even the wet, the wool provided some warmth. She was okay for the moment. Her husband and the dogs needed the cover worse.

Betty grit her teeth and started to row.

The sleet had turned to rain, the fog bank lifting. The clouds still hung low over the water, but they could see farther than this morning.

They saw the Coast Guard ship pass them by, but it was going so fast, by the time Betty was able to stand up and start waving the tarp in the air, the boat was gone. The same thing happened with the white and black hulled RCMP cutter.

"I think we're at the head waters to the inlet to Bella Coola now," Reggie stuttered.

Betty nodded and tucked her head down, pulling the oars towards her with all her might. The current was strong. The dinghy was fighting her every move.

Despair nagged at her, curling like a snake inside her stomach.

Bile rose to her throat, but she refused to give in.

We're going to make it, she chanted to herself. *We're going to make it.*

Champ raised his head and whimpered.

"It's okay, buddy," she mumbled, trying to reassure the dog.

The wind picked up, making it even harder to row. It drove against her back, causing a chill to ripple through her body.

We're going to make it.

***

"There! A boat," the tallest of the Search and Rescue crew shouted, pointing to starboard.

Benny cut the engines and let his seiner drift towards the aluminum skiff bobbing on the waves.

The dinghy was empty, the oars washed overboard.

Benny's heart sank, his hopes dashed.

"Pull her up," he ordered his men.

The crew used a hook to snag the dinghy's mooring rope and hauled the rowboat aboard.

"Anything in it," he yelled from the bridge. "Any clothes? Hat? Anything?"

"Just these beads," his first mate hollered back, lifting a beaded necklace into the air.

The necklace swung in the breeze.

Benny recognized the prayer necklace. It was a Muslim tasbih Islamic necklace made from ninety-nine wooden prayer beads. Now he knew who the families were on *The Persephone*. They were refugees from China's re-education camps just like he once was.

"*Nadon, Atlin, Salty Dawg*," Benny said into the radio. "We found a dinghy. Nothing was in it but some prayer beads. Is *The Persephone* missing her skiff?"

"Hang on, *Salty Dawg*. Over," replied the captain of the *Atlin*.

"*Salty Dawg, Nadon*," came the reply a short time later. "*Persephone*'s dinghy is still here, but we've been told there were two other dinghy's that went missing."

"Missing, yeah right," Benny hissed.

"We'll keep this one, *Nadon*, and continue to look for the other dinghy," Benny finished. "*Salty Dawg* to Fishermen's Posse, we are just north of Kwatna, approaching the end of Burke Channel."

"Roger that," came the responses over the radio.

"Heads up everyone, we gotta be close," Benny informed his crew.

***

Betty heard the tendon rip as she pushed down on the oar's handle, the wooden oar banging against the boat's side as she let go. Pain sliced through her left shoulder. She gasped, almost fainting.

"Bets, you okay," her husband shouted, tossing the tarp from his shoulders.

The dogs whined and stood up, both leaning their chests into hers to comfort her.

Tears fell from her eyes.

"I think I over did it, honey," she winced.

Reggie moved towards her, but the little dinghy rocked precariously.

White caps dotted the surface, the waves swelling around the skiff.

"I'll be okay," Betty hissed, motioning for her husband to stay put.

"It's getting too rough to be out here," he growled. "We need ta head to shore."

Betty could see he was angry with himself. Always her knight in shining armor, she thought.

"I don't think I can move," she groaned, head down so that Reggie couldn't see the full force of her pain. Not that it mattered, her left arm hung limply at her side.

Champ woofed and wagged his tail.

The Border collie sat up straighter.

A wave rocked the boat and Betty leaned sideways, sure that

she was going to be sick.

Reggie chuckled.

"I don't think it's funny," she fumed, glancing up into Reggie's steel grey eyes as she fought down the nausea. She was exhausted, wet, hands and feet so cold she couldn't feel them anymore, and starving.

"I think I've lost my sense of adventure," she hissed.

"Don't give up yet. Look," he grinned.

Betty shifted in her seat. There, on the horizon, chugging towards them at top speed was one big mother of a seiner.

The seiner blew its horn. The horn was so loud it hurt her ears.

"Fitting," Reggie chortled.

"What is," she snapped, chastising herself. She should be happy. Rescue was in sight, but the pain raking down her shoulder and through her back was making her irritable.

"That's the *Salty Dawg*, Benny Lee's boat," Reggie drawled. "You know, the fella that tried to give us the potty mouthed parrot."

Okay, Betty grinned, amused, that was funny.

"Come on, where's my girl," her husband kidded her.

Betty shook her head and rolled her eyes.

Oooh, bad idea.

The world tilted sideways. Her eyes rolled back in her head as she fell forward in a faint, grabbing hold of Champ for support at the last minute.

The seiner cruised to a stop a couple hundred yards from the skiff. The *Salty Dawg* launched a motorized boat and raced towards them.

The dogs stamped their feet and whined, tails whipping happily from side to side. Champ licked Betty's face, bringing her back to reality. The Border collie leapt onto the rescue boat as soon as it pulled up beside them.

"Yer a sight fer sore eyes," Reggie stammered.

Betty fought back tears. Damn, but she hated showing any weakness.

"Never thought you for the type that'd let the wife do all the work, Reg," Benny's first mate joked while the two Search and Rescue crew grabbed hold of the sides of the dingy and affixed a rescue line.

"That's cause ya aren't married to this one," Reggie joked back. "Ya don't ever say 'no' to her."

Betty couldn't help but laugh, even if she was quite sure she was going to fall overboard at any minute.

Men.

"We're going to tow you back to the ship," the first mate advised them. "Can you pop your oars in the holders?"

Betty nodded. She lifted the right oar and tucked it into the side of the boat but couldn't lift her left arm at all.

"Looks like you popped a tendon," one of the rescue men said. "Not surprised. You're probably dehydrated."

"You can look after her after we get back to the *Salty Dawg*," the first mate told first aid attendant. "The chop's getting worse."

"Aye, get us out of here," Reggie agreed.

Champ whined and licked Betty's face.

She leaned into the dog, pressing her face against his neck for support.

The rescue boat towed them to the seiner. Betty crumbled, her knees buckling, little dots swimming across her vision when she stood up. Strong arms wrapped around her chest and held her tight. Someone wrapped a rope around her waist, and she was hauled jerkily upwards, her feet dangling in the air, onto the deck of the rescue ship.

Betty had never felt so embarrassed in all her life. Maybe she wasn't as tough as she thought she was.

Champ greeted her with wet kisses on one side, her husband with wet kisses on the other. Tears streamed down her face. They had made it.

The men on deck all grinned as Benny Lee came down from the bridge, a huge smile on his face.

"So, Benny, ya tried to shove yer problem parrot onto us," Reggie fumed, "on me, my wife, and our friends, no less. Not ta mention, we were on our honeymoon."

Benny stopped short.

"Uh, ya, about that," he stuttered.

Reggie burst out laughing.

"I was just joshing ya," Reggie grinned. "I told Stew to deal with it."

"Mac's a great bird, he just has a way with words," Benny smiled back, his brown eyes dancing with mischief.

"Can we chat about the bird later and go someplace warm," Betty demanded. "I can't feel my feet anymore."

"Oh, right," Benny gasped. "What's the matter with you guys, get Reg and his lady inside."

Benny's crewmen shook their heads in wonder. They had been trying to do just that.

Reggie helped Betty to the cabin. The dogs jogged along behind them.

"Has anybody heard what happened to my girl yet," Reggie stuttered.

Betty winced. She wanted to say 'his girl' was right here but knew her husband was talking about *The Persephone*. She groaned inwardly. No need to be jealous of a boat. Steady, Betty, she told herself, praying all the poor souls packed into the hold were okay.

"Aye," Benny answered as a Search and Rescue crewman handed the rescued pair a cup of hot tea. "*The Persephone* has been recovered and the RCMP are dealing with the thieving buggers that stole it. Boy, those smugglers were dumb to steal your boat."

Reggie nodded as he sipped his tea, cradling his hands around the hot mug.

"What about the families," Betty barked, not meaning to sound angry, but unable to help herself. Her shoulder and upper back throbbed.

"They're okay too," Benny beamed. "The Coast Guard just updated everyone. The women and children are all safe and sound."

Betty breathe a sigh of relief. Her stomach gurgled in agreement.

God, I could eat a horse right now, Betty winced as she lifted the teacup to her lips. The hot tea burned as it went down her throat.

"Who is everyone," Reggie asked.

"We got us a posse out looking for you guys," the first mate giggled.

"A fisherman's posse," Benny cheered.

"That's marvelous," Betty quipped, "but can someone please get us something to eat. I'm starving and the dogs are too."

"I see what ya mean about the missus," the first mate said, elbowing Reggie.

"Don't kid yourselves, she's as tough as nails, my Bets," he chimed.

"I'll be nicer once I'm warm and fed," she promised Benny and his crew.

"Reggie, you want to do the honors of contacting the posse and letting 'em know you're okay," Benny asked the grizzled mountain of a man sitting before him.

Reggie looked over at his wife. Betty smiled and nodded. She couldn't stay miserable for ever.

Benny handed Reggie the radio microphone.

"*Salty Dawg* to all ya crusty old mates out there," Reggie boomed, his voice shaking with emotion. "Phoenix here. Thank y'all. We're safe and sound. Beers on me next time I see ya."

"Hallelujah," someone shouted over the radio.

The bridge crew cackled.

"*Salty Dawg, Atlin*, good to hear. God speed."

"*Salty Dawg, Coastal Salish.* Anytime my friend."

"Ya want ta say a couple of words," Reggie blushed, glancing over at his wife.

Betty nodded.

Reggie handed her the microphone.

"Thank you everyone," Betty flushed. "We wouldn't have made it without you. If anyone has the number for the folks looking for a lost Border collie, we might have him, and if anyone finds a half-blind pug, he's ours."

"*Salty Dawg, Nadon* here. We've got your pug, but he's made quite an impression with my crew. You might have a fight on your hands to get him back, Sergeant Bruce," the captain of the RCMP boat replied.

"That's Mrs Phoenix, Captain, and you don't want to mess with me and my man, we might have to sick the fisherman's posse on you," Betty replied smoothly. "Besides, you haven't slept with him yet. He snores and farts."

"Is that your husband your talking about," the Coastal Salish captain joked.

"No, Mugsy," Betty replied dryly. "Well, maybe both."

"Yes, ma'am," the captain of the *Nadon* laughed. "We'll drop Mugsy off on the way back."

Reggie hugged his wife.

Betty felt his breath on her face.

Hallelujah was the right word, although she wasn't sure if the captain had shouted 'hallelujah' that they were safe or that Reggie would buy him a beer. You never knew with these fishermen.

Tears rose in her eyes and she snuggled into Reggie's arms, her throbbing shoulder a drop in the bucket compared to the anguish that she had felt while being tossed around in the little skiff, trying to be brave, trying to be the stalwart wife and retired police officer. Right now, none of that mattered. She was alive, and so was her husband and both of the dogs.

Uninvited Guest

December 15th – early evening

Morris peered out of the cockeyed door to the prophet's cabin. The rain was quickly melting the snow that had accumulated in the last twenty-four hours. His tracks were slush. Water accumulated at the bottom of the treasure hunters' excavations.

It was time.

It was late enough that they probably weren't coming to the boat so he should be safe.

He crept out of the cabin and stood listening. All he heard was the snow sloughing off the trees and the pitter-patter of rain.

Satisfied that he was alone, he stamped down the trail to the beach, heading towards the cove behind the McDonald's farm.

Watchtower Mountain was smothered in fog. A thick mist coalesced at its base, spreading out over the valley below. The fog was a welcome sight. It would cover some of his movements.

The wild-haired goat farmer looked like he had just stepped out of the moors instead of a west coast forest. His red hair and beard were wind whipped and unkempt.

Green salal and yellowed ferns emerged from hibernation beneath his threadbare gumboots as he left the cover awarded by the trees and strode down the sandy incline to the beach.

He grinned.

He had timed it perfectly.

The tide was out, and the catamaran was beached, her anchor chain slack.

Morris jogged across the pebbly beach towards the *Polar Bear Express*. He laughed at the name. The catamaran was a beauty though, well cared for.

The taciturn man climbed up the aluminum ladder at the stern of the boat.

He slithered towards the wheelhouse, bent at the waist to appear less visible to anyone watching from shore. Not that they wouldn't have seen him running across the sandy beach to the boat, but he figured one could never be too careful.

Satisfied that he was alone, he tugged open the cabin door and stepped inside.

Shivers rippled up and down his spine.

"Ya shouldn't be doing this, Morris," he scolded himself, the reality of what he was doing sinking in. No matter how good or how bad his intentions were, it was wrong.

He stopped for a moment, indecisive, then shrugged and continued into the heart of the boat. He had to get to the bottom of these two trespassers on his island. There had been enough nastiness in the past couple of years to last him a lifetime and he was determined to protect the ones he cared about.

The kitchen was neat and tidy, the oak cabinets smooth and blemish free. One by one, Morris opened the cupboards and drawers and searched inside, careful to place everything back in its place.

So far all he had found were necessities, cans of soup, Uncle Ben's Minute Rice, cannisters of coffee, tea, and instant milk.

"There has to be something here," he muttered.

He climbed down into what he was sure was the kid's father's bunk area. A red velvet Santa suit was tossed haphazardly on the bed along with a pointy red hat and a fake beard.

"I knew it," he gasped, smacking his lips in satisfaction. "I knew something was off with their story. He's the grinch that's stealing Christmas."

Wait! If Chris was the Santa Claus thief, then his loot must be stashed here somewhere! Surely, he wouldn't take it to Tammy's cottage.

Morris tore apart Chris' bunk, looking under the mattress, inside the clothing drawers, and in the cubby hole bathroom. All he found was some costume jewelry and a four-inch by four-inch square present with a bright purple bow. The present was buried beneath a bunch of socks and underwear. The wrapping paper looked old.

Merry Christmas, Sam. Love Mom.

That was what the note said.

Funny, Morris mused, the kid had never mentioned a mother and there definitely hadn't been a woman with them at the house. There were no women's clothes in the closet either.

Morris continued to slip through the catamaran, running his fingers along crevices, looking for hidden compartments, but he came away empty.

His frustration level was growing. Time was ticking away. He was determined to find some proof that the kid and her father were thieves, but so far, all he had for evidence was the Santa Claus suit.

The boat creaked and canted sideways.

Morris was in Sam's room when he was tossed sideways into the bunk. Footsteps clunked on the deck above his head. He heard two sets: one heavy, one softer.

Darn it, he cursed himself. They were here. His timing was completely off.

"Wow, we just made it in time," he heard the little girl say to her father as she ducked inside the forward living area.

"Yep, stow the groceries, kiddo," her father replied. "Shouldn't be more than a half hour before we're afloat. The tide comes in quickly in this bay, I've noticed."

What was he going to do?

Father and daughter clumped around upstairs. Morris looked for a place to hide. The kid's quarters were cramped, but there was a tall thin closet at the foot of the bed. Thankfully, he was skinny. He should be able to fit in there, depending on how many clothes and toys she had stuffed inside.

The boat groaned as it heeled to starboard, the hull beginning to lift as the tide rose.

His mouth watered as the smell of cooking onions and vegetables assailed him, filling the cabin with a delicious scent.

"Turkey stir fry," the kid cheered. "Can you add extra Teriyaki sauce, Daddy?"

"Don't I always, sweetie?"

"Yesssss," she giggled, "but I thought a reminder wouldn't hurt."

"I can't believe you're not turkeyed out yet," her father laughed as the stir fry sizzled.

Morris tiptoed over to the closet and carefully opened the door. Relief flooded through him when nothing dropped on his head.

The unruly goat farmer pulled back. Children's t-shirts, sweaters and jeans, a bright yellow flowered rain jacket and a green elf costume, hung neatly on hangers. Two pairs of kid's runners, one set purple and the other pink, sat side by side on top of three children's board games and books...lots of books. For a kid Sam's age, there wasn't much.

Morris felt his heart sink.

This was no way for a kid to live.

No wonder she was a smarty pants.

Morris carefully pulled some clothes out of the closet, lifted the mattress and hid them beneath it. He did the same with the books and two board games, making sure that the mattress wasn't lumpy anywhere in case the kid came down for a nap or something.

He still wasn't sure what to do.

Obviously, he hadn't even considered getting caught or being stranded on the boat.

Morris heard the family, small as it was, sit down to dinner. His ears perked up when they started talking about their plans.

***

Sam was happy, not over the moon happy, but happy like when Daddy took her for dinner at a posh Italian restaurant in Vancouver for her birthday last year.

If she weren't so worried about Also, this would be the happiest day ever.

Also looked like a ghost, whited faced, brown hair limp and lifeless, lying in bed on his white sheets, in a dark room that smelled of dog, lemons, and eucalyptus.

Sam was thinking on what she could do to help him get better when her father said it was time to go.

"You know, turkey stir fry is pretty good," her father said from the other side of the dinner table.

"It's scrumpt-you-us," she declared with a giggle.

"We still have a lot of left-overs," he continued. "What do you think we should do with it tomorrow?"

"Well, we could have turkey burgers," Sam suggested.

"Or creamed turkey and corn," he added.

"Yuck," she cringed.

Her father laughed as he finished his plate of food.

"You know, I was thinking that maybe it was time to settle down. What do you think about me finding out if they want to sell the cottage?"

"Really," Sam gasped with surprise.

"Really," he grinned.

"And live on Seal Island forever and ever," she whispered, not sure if she was hearing right.

"Maybe not forever and ever, but for now," her father nodded.

Okay, now Sam was over the moon happy. She wasn't sure she should react right away. Maybe it was a trick question. She didn't know why her daddy would ask her a trick question, but in her books, kids were getting asked trick questions by witches and wizards all the time.

"I'd love to live on Seal Island, Daddy," she replied, scrunching up her nose, "but I'm not sure if I want to live in the laughing dead lady's cottage."

That was a good answer, she thought. Her father wasn't a wizard, but sometimes he had a faraway look like he wasn't there, and it scared her. He didn't have the faraway look now, but this was a weird conversation. Not weird like crazy, but weird in that he had never mentioned settling down before. In fact, he always told her that homeownership was for dummies.

"I see," her daddy stiffened.

Oh, oh, Sam realized. *Maybe she shouldn't have said that?*

"I guess if we painted it, it wouldn't be the laughing dead lady's place anymore, it would be ours," she countered.

Relief flooded through her when her father smiled.

"That's right," he agreed. "You could paint your room whatever color you wanted. Royal purple, maybe, or pink. It would be your choice."

Sam smiled. That would be fun, a pink AND purple room. She could visit Also whenever she wanted and stop in to see Mrs Tullis and eat jam and biscuits.

Dinner continued until she felt the *Polar Bear Express* drifting on its anchor chain, the hull completely submerged. It was time to go.

"Where are we going tonight, Daddy," she asked as she cleared the table and filled the sink with hot sudsy water.

"We're going to go South tonight, honey," Daddy said, donning his winter coat and slipping on his deck boots, the ones with the anti-slip soles. "It's a little too hot in Courtenay and Comox."

"That sounds like a plan," she chimed as she washed the dishes. "Can I go again?"

"Yep, I might need you to slip through a window," he finished, before heading up to the wheelhouse to weigh anchor and set off.

"Yes," Sam high-fived the air, soapy bubbles raining down upon her.

Sam giggled.

She dried the dishes and put them away and then scampered down the stairs to her bedroom. Her elf costume was still in the closet; she wanted to wear it, but it was freezing outside even though it wasn't snowing. She couldn't wear long johns underneath the outfit because she had grown too tall. A sweater over top of it would defeat the purpose, but that was what she would have to do.

She opened the clothes closet, jumping backwards as if she'd seen a mouse. Sam would have screamed except the crazy goat farmer's hand shot out faster than a speeding bullet and smothered her cry of alarm.

"Shhhh," the crazy man whispered hoarsely. "Please don't give me away."

"Hmmm. Hmmm. Hmmm," she mumbled angrily.

"If I take my hand away, do you promise not to scream?" he mumbled.

She nodded assent.

"What are you doing in my closet?" she fumed after Morris removed his hand from over her mouth.

"I'm sorry, I didn't mean ta stay that long, but then you guys came, and I had to hide," he muttered, his face turning as red as his hair.

"You didn't answer my question," she growled, hands on her hips.

"Okay, I didn't trust ya and I was worried ya'd hurt my friends," Morris replied.

Sam wasn't born yesterday. He was a liar. Yep, a real player.

"No, you weren't, you were going to steal from us," she snapped, her eyes narrowing.

For a minute, Sam thought he was going to barge past her and run upstairs. She wasn't sure what her father would do if he did. It all depended on if Daddy caught him or not.

The man went from looking terrified to guilty to annoyed all within a couple of seconds.

"All right, I was looking ta see what ya were hiding and I saw yer father's Santa suit," he mumbled. "I knows that yer father is the thief the coppers are looking fer."

Sam blanched.

"You're a bad man," she simmered, finding her courage.

"I'm not a bad man," he whined, taken aback. "I've had enough of murderers, crackpots, and thieves, is all."

The catamaran lurched forward. Waves splashed against the hull. A soft keening filled the cabin as the wind whistled through the ropes on the main mast above them. The vessel was under sail, skipping across the water on a south by southwest heading.

"It's too late for you to leave now," she whispered, panic rising into her breast. "Not unless you were a whale. If you were a whale or a seal, maybe even an otter, I could toss you overboard and you could swim to shore."

"What," Morris stuttered, horrified.

"You know I once had a goldfish. It was a big sucker and grew too big for the tiny bowl it was in. I set it free and threw it overboard. A seal popped its head out of the ocean and swallowed it. It was horrible; I cried for a week."

The man stuffed in the closet reminded her of her goldfish. His eyes were all buggy and his mouth was opening and closing rhythmically.

"Don't worry, I'm not going to do it, but Daddy might," she nodded sagely. "He wouldn't let anyone separate us. You blab and my daddy goes to jail, and I go to juvie. I know. Daddy told me so."

"Look," Morris sighed, back-peddling. "I'll make ya a deal."

"What kind of deal," she asked, knowing not to trust a player. Daddy raised her right.

"You don't tell yer pa about me being down here and I won't tell anyone about yer pa being a thief and all," he begged.

"I don't trust you," she seethed. "What do you have that I can hold to make sure you keep your word?"

Morris shook his head, not knowing what he could offer.

"All I got is my farm, my goats, and my dogs," he shrugged.

"I don't want your farm or your goats, but I'll take your dogs," she answered, "and if you break your promise, I'll tell the police you hurt me and that you're a liar."

To make a point, Sam started to whimper, hugged her arms around her chest, and forced tears to rise in the corners of her eyes, all while puffing out her lips into a quivering pout.

"Yer downright evil, child," Morris winced.

"Only if I have to be," she grinned, dropping her wounded bird act. "We got a deal?"

"Deal," Morris muttered, sticking out a hand.

Sam and the goat farmer shook on it.

"Sam, I need you to take the helm for a few minutes," her father hollered down at her.

"Stay here and out of sight," she whispered. "I really don't know what daddy would do if he finds you here."

"Coming," she yelled up the ladder, plucking a grey sweater and a windproof jacket from the closet.

With a cheeky grin, she closed the door on Morris, a smidgeon of happiness returning. Maybe she'd end up with two dogs and a house to live in if the Crazy Goat Man kept up his end of the bargain. Although, the jury was out on if she would feel comfortable living in Tammy Smith's haunted cottage.

***

Chris cruised along the shoreline, watching the light go out one by one in the waterfront houses that lined the coast between Lantzville and Departure Bay in Nanaimo. Inside a small notebook he kept track of what houses went dark precisely on the hour and the half hour. This gave him a good sign of what homeowners were probably on holiday. People made the mistake of setting the timers they bought from the hardware store to either go off at the same time on the hour or staggered them in half-hour intervals.

So far, he had seen four houses that he wanted to hit tonight and another four that he would hit the next night. They were in higher end neighborhoods. He'd have to double check his tool kit before he left. Those houses would all have alarm systems.

Chris found a nice spot to moor between Piper's Lagoon and Shack Island in Nanaimo. There were several other sailboats and cruisers tied to mooring buoys, not as many as in the summer, but enough boats for the *Polar Bear Express* to blend in.

The streetlights along Hammond Bay Road glowed orange in the light rain that was falling. It was midweek and traffic was nonexistent at this late hour. Security lights glared like cat's eyes outside of many of the upper scale houses on the hill. Inside the newer subdivisions to the south, the houses were stacked together like cord wood.

It was the older homes on the water with mature landscaping and less substantial doors and windows that interested Chris. They were much easier to break into, even with alarms.

He checked his watch. It was one a.m.

Chris entered the main cabin to find his daughter dressed in her elf uniform fast asleep on the wrap around kitchen bench seat. Her black hair framed her innocent face. The only features she shared with her mother were her chin and wide lips. His heart ached with sadness. Sam never asked about her mother or why she left them. He had done his best to make up for it. He never knew what happened to his wife or if she had ever had a change of heart. In the long run, given the life he and Sam lived, it was best if she couldn't find them.

That begged the question: once they stopped living off the grid, would Sam's mother suddenly show up and try to take Sam away from him?

Chris blanched. He'd never allow that to happen. It could though, couldn't it? Maybe he needed to rethink this settling down thing.

Chris ducked into his bedroom and climbed into the Santa suit. Four more nights to make hay while the sun shone, he figured, and then he would take his daughter to Vancouver for Christmas. He would go to the bank and open the safe deposit box and see if he had enough to purchase the cottage and decide if he really wanted to. If not that cottage, they could go looking for property on one of the smaller islands up north. He needed a quiet place where his comings and goings on the catamaran wouldn't spark interest. Seal Island was perfect, but it wasn't the only island he liked.

A muffled thump rocked the boat.

It sounded like it was coming from Sam's room.

Puzzled since his daughter was above, Chris peeked into her room, not sure what he would find. He looked around, but everything seemed in its place. Sam's clothes were on the floor. Her pajamas were piled in a corner on the bed for when they got home. A tattered copy of *The Black Stallion* lay open on her comforter, an eagle feather for a bookmark.

Chris shrugged and went upstairs.

"Sam," he whispered, placing a gentle hand on her shoulder, "it's time to go."

"Ummm," she murmured, her eyes opening. "I'm up."

Chris grinned down at her as she rubbed the sleep from her eyes.

"Wear your black raincoat and black boots tonight, it's rainy and we're in the city so nothing bright," he informed her.

"Okay, Daddy," she moaned as she stretched.

Sam stood up, grabbed her raincoat from the coat hook by the cabin's hatch and tugged on her gumboots. Her father did the same.

"Where are we," she asked quietly as they went up on deck.

Chris lowered the dingy.

"We're in Nanaimo," he replied. "See those two houses over there, that's where we're heading."

"Cool," his daughter replied, climbing down into the rowboat.

Chris rowed them to shore, the oars making a soft swishing sound in the water. The rain deadened the noise.

It was a beautiful night, despite the weather. The dampness a welcome change from the winter blast over the past few days. A light fog drifted over the lagoon.

Sam jumped into the surf when the skiff bottomed out on the sandy beach. She waited patiently when he pulled the dinghy up on shore.

Chris slipped past his daughter, his gumboots sinking deep into the sand as he strode towards the first job of the night, a delightful home with enormous bay windows overlooking Shack Island.

It only took a few minutes for Chris to bypass the alarm system; although, it proved more difficult to get inside than he expected. This was where Sam came in. He found a suitable side window and popped the glass frame out of its channel. The old aluminum framed bathroom window had been overlooked when they replaced all the others.

He lifted Sam up.

"I almost can't fit," she complained as she struggled through the narrow opening. "It's too small."

"You're just growing up, sweetie," Chris chuckled.

Sam wiggled the last of the way in, crashing to the ground on the other side.

"You okay?"

"Yeah, my foot landed in the toilet," she grumbled. "Good thing I'm wearing gumboots and not sneakers."

Chris smothered a laugh as he strode back around the house to the patio doors.

Sam slid the doors open, and they were inside.

The house was a bonanza. He privately thanked the owners for thoughtfully thinking the house was safe enough with the alarm system to leave their jewelry out. Chris even found some bonds worth five thousand dollars each with a maturity date of next year tucked haphazardly beneath an unopened package of socks in a dresser drawer.

Sam found an additional thousand dollars in cash in a side office.

It was almost too easy.

"Sam, we've got enough, let's get out of here," he announced, the hair on the back of his neck rising.

"Yes, Daddy," she whispered, following him to the door.

That was what he loved about his daughter. She never complained, especially when they were on a job.

They slipped out the patio doors and into the night.

The night was so quiet that every sound traveled. A squelch of tires on wet pavement echoed through the night.

Chris hustled his daughter to the rowboat.

"I thought we were going to hit that house too," she whispered, pointing to the two-story house a couple of lots down.

"I got a bad feeling," he mumbled, pushing the dinghy into the water.

They were almost to the catamaran when the lights from a car pulling off the road and into the side street entrance where the house was located illuminated the waterfront. The car pulled into the drive at the front of their latest job.

Chris steered the dinghy around to the stern of the boat and warned Sam with a finger in front of his mouth to be quiet. Sound over water would travel even in the rain.

Sam climbed aboard the catamaran and disappeared quickly into the darkened cabin. Chris tied up the dinghy and padded quietly after his daughter, keeping to the shadows the mast and folded sails offered.

"Change into your pajamas quickly in case the police pay us a call," he ordered her. "Make sure you don't turn on any lights."

"You think the police might board our boat," she cried, eyes wide with terror. "Shouldn't we leave?"

"No, we don't to. We want to make sure that if the police send a harbor patrol boat out, we look like we were sleeping," he consoled her.

"Oh, got it," she nodded and disappeared below decks.

Chris quickly slipped out of the Santa suit and stuffed it inside a cupboard below his bed. He pulled on his own set of flannel pajamas and messed up his sheets and blankets. He then crept back upstairs and watched as the lights went on inside the beach house.

An angel must be looking out for them, he thought as several police cars arrived in a hail of gravel and wail of sirens. They made a heck of a racket.

Lights popped on in the cabins of the boat beside him and the sailboat three over from him.

Ahhh, live-aboards, he grinned. *God bless them.*

The price of housing was so high on Vancouver Island now that many people lived on their boats or in RV's. Some lived this way by choice, not wanting to be strangled by a mortgage or tied down by homeownership, but most were due to financial constraints. He wouldn't exactly qualify for a mortgage, not with his occupation. It begged the question – should he buy a house even if he had enough?

This was going to be a harder decision that he imagined. He

could simply register Sam for homeschool.

Chris waited until for the perfect moment to flick on the cabin lights, grab a coat and wander up onto the deck.

"What in God's name is going on over there," a man asked him from the neighboring boat.

"No idea," Chris answered.

Like him, the man on the next boat wore a rain slicker over pajamas, gumboots on his feet.

"Sure are a lot of police cars," he said.

"I'll say," Chris agreed. "Maybe someone got hurt or died or something?"

"I don't see any ambulances," the man nodded. "Robbery, you think?"

"Could be," Chris answered.

"You guys know what's going on," a woman shouted from across the water.

"No," Chris shouted back. "Do you?"

"No idea," she returned. "I expect we'll find out later or tomorrow when the harbor patrol stops by."

"Yeah, you're probably right," Chris agreed.

"So much for a quiet night's sleep," the man on the boat beside him moaned.

"Yeah, I'm going back to bed," Chris waved. "Not my problem."

"Me too," the man said and disappeared below decks.

"See you in the morning," Chris shouted to the woman.

She lifted a hand in acknowledgement and then she too went back inside.

Chris smothered a laugh as he turned off the cabin's lights.

"Everything okay," his daughter asked, peeking out her bedroom door.

"Fine, sweetie, but we're done for the night," he smiled, reassuring her. "I've stashed everything away. Tomorrow, we'll play dumb if the police boat stops by."

Sam shot him a thumbs-up and ducked her head back inside her cabin.

***

"Police," Morris stuttered, carefully opening the closet door. "What are we gonna do?"

"I got an idea," Sam whispered fiercely. "Once the cop cars are gone and Daddy is asleep, I'll row you to shore or over to one of the other boats. You can borrow a dinghy and row yourself to shore."

"What'll I do from there," he gasped. "How will I get home?"

"Duh, that's your problem, you're the one who sneaked onto our boat," Sam replied scornfully. "Take a bus, hitch a ride, call someone. Just make sure that you don't tell them about us."

"Right," he agreed. "That makes sense. I'll tell folks I missed the ferry. Stew or someone will pick me up at the marina."

Sam rolled her eyes. She was only nine, but even she knew what to do if she got separated from her father: con her way home. It never occurred to Sam that made her more of a player than the frightened man crouched in her closet.

"Ya know, yer pretty smart fer a kid," Morris grumbled as he closed the closet door.

Sam snuggled down in her bed. She flipped on a tiny penlight and picked up her book. She had to make sure she didn't fall asleep. If the police came and searched their boat, it wouldn't do to find the goat farmer hiding in her bedroom.

"Sam," Morris whispered.

"Yes, Morris," she whispered back.

"I don't have any money for a bus," he confessed.

"Don't worry, there's a change purse in a drawer in the kitchen," she replied with a shake of her head. "I'll give you some."

Some people just weren't meant to be thieves.

In for a Penny

December 16th – late afternoon

"Look, it's too dangerous, Sam," her father argued. "I'll be gone a couple of days and then when I come back, we'll pack up and head to Vancouver for Christmas."

"But I want to come with you," she sobbed. "I don't want to be alone here."

"You can go visit your friend," he soothed her.

"I know but I want to come with you," Sam whined, knowing she wasn't getting anywhere. Once her father made up his mind, he was stubborner than she was. This morning she had decided to surprise him by giving him the gold coin she found. The double eagle was burning a hole in her pocket; at least, that was what it felt like to Sam.

"You know I love you, right," he crooned, kneeling in front of her.

"I do," she whispered, wrapping her arms around him. "I don't want you to go. The laughing dead lady told me in my dreams that we should leave here."

Chris wiped his daughter's tears away with his shirt cuff.

"I know you had a rough time, what with the police popping by the boat early this morning, but nothing bad happened, did it?" Chris reasoned.

Sam hated it when her daddy was right.

After Crazy Goat Man rowed to shore in a rowboat that she and Morris pinched off a powerboat moored in the lagoon, Sam had returned to the catamaran only to find that she couldn't sleep. She worried that Crazy Goat Man would snitch. That was how she thought of him now, Crazy Goat Man.

What if the police had someone hiding in the bushes on shore and they saw her?

What if Crazy Goat Man talked?

What if Daddy went to jail and never told them about her? How would she live? She would be all alone, an orphan, like Oliver Twist.

"Stop it, Sam, I can see your mind whirring," Daddy warned her.

"Yeah, it is," she sniffled.

"If I'm not back in two days and you're really worried, I want you to go to Mrs Tullis," Chris told his daughter.

"Why her," Sam asked, surprised by her father's earnestness. For a moment, she set aside all thoughts of Brother Twelve's coin and her tale of how she found it.

"Because she's a nice lady and she'll look after you," her father said. "Tell her I went to a job interview in the city. You'll think of something, you're one of the most creative kids I know. If you aren't here when I get back, then I know you're with Mrs Tullis."

"But if I lie to her, won't that make me a player?"

"No, it makes you a survivor, sweetie," her daddy grinned.

Sam felt better. She didn't want to lie to the nice jam lady, and she never wanted to be a player like Crazy Goat Man.

Speaking of Crazy Goat Man, she supposed that on the way to visit Also, she should make sure he got back home and go get her new dogs.

"Daddy, can I have some money before you leave to go to the store," she asked her father innocently, knowing that he would say 'no'. He always did. This time, though, she could magically pull the coin from her pocket and tell him 'Ooh, I forgot, I already have money'. Wouldn't that be funny?

"Sure," Chris said, standing up. He pulled out his wallet and handed her twenty dollars. "If you need more there is an emergency stash of twenties in the nightstand by my bed."

Sam couldn't hide her surprise. Her father tussled her hair. This wasn't going at all as Sam had planned.

She hugged her father one last time before he left and waved to him as he strode down the road, heading for the *Polar Bear*

Express. She still didn't like him leaving so fast. In fact, she had a bad feeling that she might not see her daddy again. To top it all off, she still hadn't been able to show him the coin in her pocket.

Sam chewed on her lower lip. Daddy never left a stash of emergency cash and never told her to go see a stranger, even if Mrs Tullis wasn't really a stranger, if she was afraid. It didn't make her feel all warm and fuzzy inside.

Sam's tummy did a flip-flop as her father's lanky figure vanished into the trees at the end of the road.

"I love you, Daddy," she whispered.

Sam heard a loud snort and the clickety-clack of hooves on gravel. She whirled around and saw Gertrude and Peaches wandering down the road.

She quickly slipped on a raincoat and boots and slammed the door shut behind her as she raced over to give the pig and cow a hug.

"Hey, Gertie. Hello, Peaches," she laughed as she hugged each in turn. "Want to come with me to Crazy Goat Man's place. I need to see if he's home yet and go get my new dogs. They aren't really my new dogs, but that's a long story."

The pot-bellied pig and Jersey cow followed her as she wandered down the road, one hand slapping the coalescing water drops from the bushes she passed. It was a warm day for December.

Sam was glad of the animals' company; they lightened the sullen mood the morning had wrought upon her. There was no point wasting daylight crying in her room, anyway.

She waved to Mrs Tullis as she skipped by her house, not knowing if the senior had seen her or not. It just seemed the right thing to do in case she saw Sam through the window.

She slowed as she approached Morris' driveway. Knowing nothing about goats, she was too afraid to go in.

Sam whistled shrilly for the dogs.

"Puppies," she called up the lane. "Hello, big and little guy."

The little girl laughed lightly. She knew the Saint Bernard was Brutus but didn't know what the collie's name was.

Disappointment seemed to be the order of the day as no dogs answered her call.

Gertrude nosed her pocket, causing her to stagger backwards a couple of feet.

"Stop that, silly pig," Sam laughed, retrieving the inside of her coat pocket from the pig's mouth. Good thing the prophet's coin was in her pant pocket or it would be in Gertrude's belly by now.

"Either Crazy Goat Man made it home and locked his dogs in his house or he had someone pick them up," she informed her four-legged friends. "Guess we'll go see Also, Gertie. I have to pop down to the store too. I really need some milk."

Sam danced down the road, spinning like a top every so often for no other reason than she could. She giggled and laughed and stuck out her tongue to catch raindrops. Her two buddies quickly lost interest and reversed course, heading back up South Shore Road. Sam was so preoccupied with catching raindrops that she didn't notice she was alone until she stopped in front of Ida and Also's house.

Sam walked up the drive.

A chorus of woofs sounded off in the back yard. Also's two puppies pushed their way between all the others and greeted her at the side gate. She thought she saw the Crazy Goat Man's dog running in the back yard, but there were so many Saint Bernard's that looked alike she couldn't be sure.

She gave up, ruffled the puppies' heads through the fence and then knocked on the front door.

"Hi, Mrs Abercrombie, is Also doing better," she asked Ida when the salt and pepper haired woman answered the door.

"He is," Ida replied warmly. "As a matter of fact, he is eating the last bowl of turkey soup I made thanks to you."

Sam's grin was as wide as the Grand Canyon as she entered the house.

"Is that my friend Sam," she heard Also call hopefully from his bedroom as she hustled down the hall. "I heard someone knock."

"It's me," Sam laughed, her eyes bright, as she greeted her friend.

Also sat up in bed, a coloring book in his lap, and a tray with an empty soup bowl on the nightstand.

"Knock. Knock," Also smiled.

"Who is there," Sam responded, jumping up on the corner of the bed and making herself comfortable.

"Icing."

"Icing who," she giggled.

"Icing so loud, the neighbors can hear," Also laughed and then broke into a fit of coughs.

"Also is still not out of the woods yet so maybe keep your visit short again today, Sam," Ida suggested, standing in the doorway.

"Okay," Sam beamed.

Sam wondered why Also's auntie just said he wasn't out of the woods yet. What did that mean? Also looked all right. His face wasn't bedsheet white anymore and he was able to talk, but he did wheeze a lot.

"I'm so glad you came to see me," the boy in the bed confessed. "No one does, not when Also is sick. They get all sad and go away."

"I'd say I won't go away, but Daddy said we're going to the city for Christmas like we do every year," Sam informed him after turning her head to make sure his auntie had left the room. "Daddy says he is going to see if we can afford to buy the laughing lady's house. If we can, we can see each other all the time."

Also laughed and clapped his hands. Once again, the laughter turned into a coughing fit. His chest gurgled when he did so. He motioned to Sam for water and she quickly handed him the glass of water from the table beside her.

"That's better," he said after he had a drink.

"What's wrong with you, Also," Sam asked, concerned. "You are going to get better, aren't you?"

"Angel says I will, so I will," he mumbled.

Sam didn't ask him about what angel told him so or if the angel was still here. She looked around and didn't see any, but maybe the angel was only visible to Also.

Suddenly, Sam knew what would make her friend feel better.

It was kismet. Daddy taught her that word and she loved it. Kismet.

"Also, do you remember when we went treasure hunting the day we met," she whispered, leaning forward.

He nodded, his face so beautiful that Sam felt a tingling in her toes that grew and grew, travelling all the way up her body until she felt her worries of the morning and the night before evaporating.

Kismet.

Sam tugged the coin out of her jean pocket, picked the lint off it and handed it to Also.

"I found this," she stammered. "I went back in the middle of the night and dug it up. It was stuck in the roots of the tree where Crazy Goat Man's dog was digging. I want to give it to you for good luck."

"Sam," Also croaked, tears welling in his eyes. "It's beautiful, but you can't give away the treasure that you found."

"Yes, I can," she nodded. "It's mine to give and I want you to have it. When I'm not here, you can hold it in your hand and think of me and the adventures we'll have together when I get back after Christmas. That way, we will always be close. You have to keep it secret though."

Also leaned forward and hugged Sam. Sam hugged him fiercely back. She prayed that she wasn't playing Also. He didn't deserve that. In her heart, she believed she would return to Seal Island. Daddy was Daddy, so she wasn't completely sure.

"Okay, you two, that's enough visiting for now," Ida smiled as she came into the room.

Also immediately hid the coin beneath his pillow.

"I'll stop by and see you tomorrow," Sam chimed.

Also smiled and pulled the covers up to his chin.

Sam knew he would keep their little secret. Except for her father, she had never given anybody anything before. It felt good.

***

"In for a penny, in for a pound," Morris muttered to himself as he dragged himself off the ferry.

He was lucky to have caught it. Upon arriving by bus at the marina on the big island, he discovered that the ferry was doing an unscheduled trip because the engine had broken down the day before and lots of folks besides him were stranded waiting to get home.

Morris walked by The Bristling Boar and thought of stopping at the pub for a pint, but his back ached from the hours spent cramped inside Sam's closet plus he hadn't slept a wink in over twenty-four hours, and he needed to feed his animals. Ida had graciously agreed to retrieve his dogs when he phoned early this morning and explained that he was stuck on Vancouver Island. She never asked why he was there.

All anyone talked about on the ferry was the Santa Claus thief and Reggie and Betty's brush with death at the hands of human traffickers.

Morris was glad that they were unharmed, but it wasn't like it was drug smugglers who took over Reggie's ship. He had already heard from one of the bus drivers that the group was Chinese refugees. Apparently, the imam hired a group of sailors off the docks in Beijing to smuggle them into Canada.

What a crazy thing to do, he mused as he made his way home.

Regardless, his friends were safe, and it was now he who was in a quandary. There were decisions to make. He knew who the Santa Claus thief was but had promised the girl he wouldn't say anything. She was right. If they arrested her father, they would send her to juvie and from there to a foster or group home.

Morris got into a lot of trouble as a kid and went to juvie twice. It was no cake walk, but he was a tough kid and had parents, a sister, and a place to come home to. Sam was smart, but she was all alone in the world. What would happen to her? She'd end up shunted around from group home to group home in the foster system until she was eighteen and then turned out onto the street.

"Darned kid," he grumbled.

For better or for worse, he'd keep her secret just so that she didn't end up in the system.

The alpine goats bleated loudly and gamboled around him as he entered the yard. Morris couldn't help but laugh. The little goats were such characters. After he cared for his menagerie, including the hens in the hen house and the handful of Muscovy ducks he had purchased from Rainbow, he would retrieve his dogs and maybe go check on the girl. It all depended on if her father were home.

***

Chris rowed back out to the catamaran. He felt awful leaving Sam by herself once again, but if he wanted to provide a permanent home for them, he had to continue. She needed stability. His mind was made up. They'd buy a house and settle down. It was time to step up to the plate.

The police couldn't have known it was the Santa Claus thief who hit the house in Nanaimo last night. The house's security system hadn't included cameras. If they had suspected him or one of the other two people living on their boats, the police would have boarded and searched each boat in turn instead of simply questioning everyone. The mature lady on the sailboat and their immediate neighbor inadvertently gave him an alibi.

"Yes officer, the commotion awakened us. We all were out on deck in our pajamas wondering what was going on," and "nope, didn't see anyone, just my neighbors here,".

Chris hummed an old ZZ Top tune as he climbed the ladder onto his boat and tied the dinghy down. Two more nights to go, one if the money house yielded him a good profit, then he and Sam would be off to Vancouver. Maybe they'd take in a show. Sam loved *The Nutcracker*. It was a Christmas tradition.

He made his way to the wheelhouse and pulled the pocket-sized notepad from his breast pocket. There were three houses on his list from last night. The one that he was most interested in was an architectural marvel or a nightmare, depending on how much one loved concrete, glass and steel. That was the one he would hit first.

Chris started the engine and headed out to sea. He would moor the catamaran amidst the boats off Protection Island and row into shore. It would be a longer haul, but much safer, as last night had proven. There definitely was safety in numbers.

Murphy's Law

December 17th - wee hours

One a.m.

Chris slithered along the sidewall of the multi-level cement and glass walled monolith tucked into the cliff overlooking the strait. He was sweaty from the lengthy row from Protection Island to the waterfront home, but it was a necessary evil as it was the closest place for him to moor that wouldn't look conspicuous.

His Santa Claus hat bobbed against his shoulder. Sweat beaded his upper lip beneath the white beard.

This house had security cameras and light sensors triggered by movement which he stealthily navigated to avoid triggering.

There was no rain or fog to cover his movements. The stars twinkled in the night sky. The space station buzzed overhead, blinking orbs marking its progress.

Chris crept through the darkness looking for the security system's wiring. He was hoping he could find a connection box outside. It was too sophisticated a system to try breaking in and disabling from the inside. If he couldn't cut the power to the system or the house safely, he would have to walk away.

In the back of his mind something told him that he should move on. This job was too dangerous. There were too many unknowns. His gut told him that he would hit the motherload if he made it inside.

Chris discovered what he was looking for, a small grey box tucked under the cable and phone connection system. He donned a pair of rubber gloves and pulled out the necessary tools to disable them all.

He stood up and sneaked back around the house to the door leading into the garage. Sure enough, the camera lights were dark. The only light still working was a separate motion detector light on a battery which was easy to avoid.

Chris popped the deadbolt on the door, took a deep breath and using a narrow penlight made his way into the house.

There was an elegant pine Christmas tree in the living room with numerous small presents and two giant ones beneath it. The sweet scent of pine filled the air; the tree was real, not a synthetic monstrosity. Colorful ornaments dangled from its limbs. The strings of Christmas LED lights wrapped around it were dark. Chris fought the urge to turn them on.

He quickly plopped the smaller of the presents into his loot bag. They made a hollow rustling sound as they fell to the bottom of the bag. He picked up a couple of boxes. They were heavy, maybe electronics. Those too went into the bag.

Dressed in the Santa Claus outfit, Chris slipped through the house. He had left his boots on but wiped them carefully on the mat by the door. He had replaced his rubber gloves with leather ones.

The first level of the house proved fruitless, the presents being the only thing worth taking. He slowly climbed the stairs to the second level.

Inside what appeared to an office/studio, he found a large Apple iPad, a google laptop, and a podcast set-up complete with a USB mixer, two expensive microphones, pop filters and stands. Several guitars hung on pegs on the walls, an acoustic, an electric and some weird combinations of both. Chris wasn't an expert. There were also wall mounted speakers around the room too big for him to bother unhooking and carrying away.

"Hey there, I'm a rock star, put my Santa on and go play," he sang, butchering the words to Smashmouth Mason's hit song, *Hey There, You're a Rock Star*.

He scuttled back into the guest bedroom on the same floor and snatched the pillowcases from the pillows and returned to the office. After wrapping the microphones, mixer and the iPad inside the pillowcases, he carefully placed them at the bottom of the green velvet loot bag that he had borrowed from his daughter. It seemed fitting as he would give her all of these for Christmas. She'd love it, maybe even start her own podcasting journal from the deck of the *Polar Bear Express*.

Chris' penlight beam flashed over the staircase leading to the upper level of the house. His heart rate increased as he climbed the stairs and approached the master bedroom. This was where his big score should be.

The thin beam of light flickered over the bed and across the man and woman sleeping in its eyes. The woman shot straight up, looked straight at him, and screamed.

"What," the man shouted, waking instantly.

Chris bolted for the stairs.

He had been sure the house was empty. The lights had gone off house-wide at the same time just like they had when he first studied the house. It never occurred to him that the house was a Smart House.

"Stop right there Santa or I'll shoot," the half-naked man yelled as he raced down the stairs in hot pursuit.

Shoot, Chris thought as he continued to flee.

A shot rang out.

The bullet hit Chris in the side, blazing a wide hole in the red velvet. He staggered but never stopped running.

He heard a muffled scream as the man missed the last stair and tumbled to the ground.

Chris bolted through the side door and staggered to the dinghy. He threw the loot bag into the back of the boat and shoved off, ignoring the pain that ripped through his side as he leapt into the boat and started to row.

There's a special place in Hell for guys who shoot Santa, Chris fumed.

Chris hauled on the oars. Blood dribbled down his side, soaking his long johns and pants. The wound needed tending but he had to get away first.

He heard shouts in the night, but the tide was with him and despite the dizziness that threatened to topple him over the side of the boat, he was making good time.

Satisfied that he was far enough away from the noise of the police sirens and the shooter in the house, he pulled up the oars and drifted on the current.

He pulled out the emergency medical kit he stowed under the rear seat and rifled through the supplies. The penlight was useless to examine the wound; he didn't dare use it lest it be seen by some sharp-eyed officer on shore.

He groaned in pain as he used his fingers to feel the wound and dab disinfectant on it. The bullet seemed to have gone right through him.

Chris bound his waist with a large tensor bandage, gritting his teeth against the agony that enveloped him. Passing out wasn't an option.

The red-faced man in the candy apple suit, searched deep inside his soul, and soldiered on. Thoughts of a black-haired girl asleep in bed in a cottage on an island somewhere to the north of him kept him going. Leaving Sam was not an option.

***

The little girl in question moaned in her sleep. Her one-hundred-and-fifty-pound furry guardian lurched to his feet and snuffled her face. He was met with a frightened gasp as the child pulled away from him. The dog leaned forward and kissed her awake.

"Oh, Brutus, yuck," Sam whimpered, wiping the drool from her cheek.

That was the cue he was waiting for.

The dog climbed onto the bed and stretched out beside Sam, pushing her body into the wall and laying his head beside hers on the pillow. Whatever was bothering the girl, he would protect her.

Sam grinned and threw an arm over the dog.

The Border collie at her feet shifted position to accommodate everyone.

Within a moment, she was fast asleep, her breathing settling into an even rhythmic beat.

Brutus licked his lips and closed his eyes.

***

The Persephone chugged around the point leading to the marina and ferry dock, Reggie at the helm, Betty standing beside him sipping a tea and Bailey's.

The couple was exhausted, black rings circled their eyes, and their movements were sluggish.

The pug slept comfortably in Betty's arms as she leaned against the wall for support. The German shepherd and Border collie were wrapped around each other, sleeping peacefully, none the worse for wear for their adventure.

The Border collie's owners had been located thanks to the radio operator at Alert Bay. The happy dog owners were boating in from Vancouver in two days, thrilled that their collie had been rescued, even though it was by a human smuggler with a love for canines.

It turned out that the smugglers really weren't smugglers at all. They were four fisherman who had a bad year and needed the money. They were in the wrong place at the right time and got in way over their heads. Even though that was the official story, Betty thought otherwise. Two of them were far too violent to be simple fishermen.

It wasn't her problem anymore. Someone else at Head Office would investigate the smugglers' stories. Hammerton or Powder were sure to tell her the outcome of the investigation once completed.

"Ya want ta head home or ya want ta sleep here," Reggie murmured to his wife as he pulled up to the dock.

"Here, I'm too tired to walk up the hill," she sighed.

"Sounds good ta me," he croaked. "I'll go tie her up. Just go downstairs and take yerself ta bed."

Betty nodded, not having the strength to offer to help. She

was grateful that her husband was still capable. They had thought of stopping on one of the islands but agreed that they just wanted to get home.

The tired fifty-five-year-old woman slipped below deck, tucked the sleepy-eyed pug into a round bed specially made for him, and peeled off her clothes.

The sheets were clean and warm. She sighed contentedly as she pulled them up to her chin and closed her eyes.

The cabin and hold were scrubbed clean of the refugees and smugglers' scents thanks to a thoughtful group of Reggie's friends in Alert Bay. Betty smiled, remembering the ring of women with buckets, bleach and washcloths who had met them at the dock. Three men had stood alongside the women with boxes filled with smoked salmon and tidbits for the dogs.

How lucky they were, Betty realized, to have friends like that and an adventure with a happy ending.

Her husband joined her shortly. He disrobed and snuggled up beside her. His hair smelled of apple shampoo. His beard was scratchy against her face, but she didn't care.

The collie whose name she couldn't remember climbed onto the bed and curled up by her feet. She didn't mind. In truth, she would miss the dog, but was happy that its owners were pleased to get it back.

She had a couple of days to think about the collie they had named Splash. The smugglers hadn't traversed the coastal section of the West Coast Trail where the harbor master in Alert Bay told them the dog was lost. She hadn't had the chance to ask the Boss Man, as Reggie called him, where they picked up the two dogs. The same with the Pitbull who she hadn't had a chance to meet. Maybe she'd call Tom Powder and see if he could look into it before handing over the dog.

Within minutes, her husband was snoring more loudly than the pug. Betty closed her eyes and quickly followed suit.

Three a.m.

Gertrude dug for truffles beneath the old oak tree whose

moss-covered branches overhung the prophet's cabin. Peaches stood on the sod roof mowing what was left of the long summer grass.

Above them, the stars winked out as clouds drifted in, blanketing the night. A smattering of rain fell to the ground. The temperature was balmy, the cold snap moving on as the warmer waters of the Gulf Stream drifted north.

An animal crashed through the brush.

Gertrude looked up, a rotting black truffle in her mouth, as the man staggered forward dragging a bag behind him. He fell against the cabin's door, his head drooping forward.

The man didn't smell right. Even from here, the scent of blood and sweat emanated from the sickly figure.

The pot-bellied pig snorted and waddled over to him. He slapped her snout away. Gertrude squealed, not liking this at all.

The man disappeared into the cabin.

The pig heard a loud bang. Despite his rudeness, she stuck her head through the doorway and saw the man dressed in red on the floor, the bag he had been carrying ripped open. Colorful boxes of all different shapes and sizes where scattered about.

An ear-splitting boom filled the room as the roof exploded and her friend Peaches plummeted down from the ceiling, landing upon the brightly colored man and packages, knocking the door closed in the process.

Peaches bawled in fear.

The man screamed in agony.

Gertrude squealed, equally alarmed.

Search and Rescue

December 17th – afternoon

Betty and Reggie awoke to a banging on the cabin door.

"Betty are you up," her father called, continuing the din.

"We're up, Pops," she called.

"Awfully early ta be waking us," Reggie groaned, wrestling the bed linen away and sitting up.

"It's after lunch," Betty grinned, checking the time of her cell phone. "Where's the collie?"

"Oh, I let him out earlier. He and Champ needed ta go do their business. I expect Champ is showing him around."

The pug snorted and rolled over, not wanting to be bothered.

Betty climbed over her husband, tossed on a sweater and some pants, and went up to greet her father.

"What's up," she asked the rumpled old man standing before her holding a cup of coffee in each hand.

"I know you just got back, but Gertrude came home alone last night, and we can't find Peaches," he stuttered, handing her a coffee. "Gertie's off her feed too. I think something's happened."

"I'm sure Peaches is about somewhere," Betty sighed, and then took a sip of coffee. It was bitter and black but hit the spot all the same. "Weren't they staying at the farm?"

"I called Rainbow first thing. Peaches isn't there. She's not at your place, Vi's, Reggie's or Pearl's. No one has seen her since yesterday."

"That is a worry then, isn't it," Reggie said, emerging from the cabin, a disgruntled pug wrapped in one arm.

"Who's that," Archie asked, one eyebrow shooting up.

"Mugsy," Reggie replied, handing the dog to Betty and pinching her coffee cup. "Found him abandoned on a beach."

"Well that ain't right," Archie hissed.

"He's a Phoenix now," Betty grinned and then kissed the dog on the forehead. The pug farted, its tongue lolling out to one side of its wicked overbite. "And he needs a walk."

Reggie chuckled and took the pug back. He slipped out of the cabin and vaulted from the trawler to the slippery dock in a single bound.

Betty chuckled as she watched her husband place the small dog onto the dock and urge him to do his business, the pug looking none too pleased. If that had been Betty, she would have gone ass over tea kettle.

"I'm sorry, I shouldn't have pestered you," her father moaned.

"It's okay, pops, of course you should have. Peaches is one of the family. Let me make Reggie and I some breakfast and then we'll go looking for her," Betty said, giving her father a one-armed hug.

"That's marvelous," he sighed with relief. "Oh, whose Border collie is that with Champ? It didn't look like Morris'. The two of them were having a gay old time."

"We call him Splash because of the splash of white on his nose. I can't remember his real name. Anyway, his owners are coming in a couple of days to pick him up. They lost him on the West Coast Trail. He was on the smuggler's ship. Don't know how they got him."

"Huh, you guys have all had a time of it, haven't you," Archie grunted. "Right, I'll make a few more phone calls and get back to you if anyone has seen our cow."

"Righto," Betty nodded.

Her stomach let out a long, low growl.

"Eat, Angel-puss, you look like you need it," her father grinned, not looking as harried as he did when she first saw him.

Betty strode into the main cabin and turned on the coffee pot. She then set about scrambling eggs, chopping a couple of green onions, and making toast. Just as she placed the scrambled eggs with green onion bits sprinkled on top and two pieces of toast on a plate, Reggie came in.

"Yer never gonna believe it, Bets," he grinned, "but ya know that parrot of Benny's?"

"What about it?"

"Rainbow's got it trained for sing-alongs at the pub. Mac-Wednesdays, they call it," he laughed. "Apparently, the bird's a real hit. Stew can't thank us enough for not wanting it."

Betty's laugh tinkled through the cabin.

"That is good news, but eat up, we've got us a cow to hunt down," she advised. "Wait a minute where's Mugsy?"

"Oh, yer pa took him home to meet Vi," he replied, sitting down at the table and stabbing the scrambled eggs with a fork.

"Well, there goes Mugsy," she said, sitting down at the table.

"Why's that," her husband mumbled through a mouthful of egg.

"We're never going to see him again except at family get-togethers," she huffed. "I guarantee it."

"Well, we won't have to smell his farts in the middle of the night anymore," Reggie joked.

Betty smacked him in the arm, not knowing how she felt about losing the pug to Vi and her father. She had grown attached to the little guy. In the end, she guessed she'd let the pug decide.

***

Sam answered the knock on the door. She was surprised to see Crazy Goat Man standing there holding a bucket full of dog food.

Brutus woofed a greeting. Max circled him.

"Yer pa still not back," Morris mumbled, brushing past her into the house.

The goat farmer was always jittery, Sam thought. She wondered if it was just around her or if he was like that with everyone.

"Tomorrow, maybe the next day," Sam reported.

"There's enough dog food in there for another two days. Just split it up," Morris said, depositing the steel bucket on the kitchen counter.

Sam yawned. She had spent the day watching movies after a fitful night. Right now, she was watching an old Disney movie, *Homeward Bound*, and wanted to get back to it. Still, she appreciated the dog food. Brutus' appetite was as gigantic as he was. Max was self-suffering and polite.

"What about you? Ya got enough ta eat," Crazy Goat Man asked her.

Sam nodded as the Saint Bernard sniffed the bucket on the counter.

"Is that a 'yes' or a 'no," Morris pressed her.

"Yes, thank you," she responded politely.

"Okay, then," he rumbled, heading back towards the door with a quick pat for the humongous dog at his side. "If'n ya need anything, just pop down to my place or Pearl's."

"I will," Sam agreed without hesitation. It was funny how the two of them didn't really like each other at first, but things had changed. Crazy Goat Man seemed okay. The police hadn't shown up and carted her away, so that was a good thing.

"Oh, by the way, ya haven't seen Peaches have ya," he asked before leaving.

"Not since yesterday, why?"

"Appears she's gone missing," he nodded. "Not like her to stray far from Gertie. Her ma is back from her honeymoon so don't be alarmed if Betty and her beau, a bear of a man with grey hair and a beard, stop by."

Sam inhaled sharply.

Did the goat farmer tell on her after all?

"Don't get yer knickers in a twist," Morris laughed as if reading her mind. "If'n they see someone in Tammy's cottage, they're bound to knock on the door. They're good people. Ya don't need to worry."

Sam smirked. This could spell trouble for her and her father. Wasn't Gertrude and Peaches owner a retired police officer? Ugh.

"Brutus and Max thank you for the food, Morris," she added, escorting Morris to the door.

Morris waved a hand over his head and was off, heading for home.

Sam tugged at her lower lip as she returned to the chair in the living room where she had snuggled up with a glass of milk, a bag of peanut butter cookies, and a blanket. The movie rumbled on. She picked up the remote and rewound it to the place where she had been when Morris walked in.

The Saint Bernard snuffled her hand while the Border collie slept on one end of the couch. She automatically handed Brutus a cookie.

Before long, she was asleep in the chair, the movie forgotten, the Saint Bernard stretched out on the couch beside his pal, his head propped on a pillow so he could see outside.

***

Chris' eyes flickered open. The gunshot wound in his side throbbed painfully. Fever coursed through his body. His chest felt like there was two hundred pounds on it. Every muscle and joint in his body ached, plus there was a warm breeze blowing directly on his face that faintly smelled of grass and clover.

For a minute he thought he was hallucinating until his eyes came into focus and he realized there was a cow laying spread-eagled on the floor between him and the door, her face and right shoulder resting against his chest.

The cow let out a sad 'mooooo', a wail so pitiful that it would have broken his heart if he weren't so afraid. If the cow got up, she'd rake a hoof across his already battered body.

"Easy, girl," he croaked, trying his best to sooth the beast. "It's all right. Everything's just peachy."

Peaches turned towards him, her breath soft and hot against his fevered cheeks.

"Well, that explains the breeze," he mumbled to himself.

He tried to slip his arm and shoulder out from beneath the Jersey cow, but he was pinned solidly beneath her. If he cried out for help, the cow might panic, and it would be all over for him.

Water splattered into his face. He glanced upwards. The sky

183

above him was filled with dark storm clouds.

"That's just not right," he groaned as he stared at the giant hole in the roof. The cow had been on the roof when the rafters gave way.

Chris would have laughed, but the idea of dying from a cow falling on top of him didn't seem very funny when you were the one lying bleeding beneath it.

A wave of dizziness canted his world sideways. Large raindrops hit him in the face, bouncing off his nose and forehead. The rain stung as it fell harder and faster.

The cow bawled, scrambling to get up to get away from the waterfall that cascaded down upon them from above.

Chris wailed as the cow's hoof and shoulder plunged into the wound on his side. His mind spiraled away into darkness before he had a chance to whisper a prayer.

***

Betty and Reggie trudged up South Shore Road. The shepherd and the collie sniffed the bushes as they went. Archie, Vi, Rainbow and Frank McDonald were scouring North Shore Road and the acreages along it. Melinda, Reggie's manager, and some of his staff were searching the waterfront and Mountain Road.

Gertrude walked along behind them, neither slowing them down nor assisting in the search of her friend. Instead, the pot-bellied pig shuffled along, head weaving from side to side.

"There's something wrong with Gertrude," Reggie said, stopping to examine the dejected pig.

"I know," Betty agreed. "Dad says she's been like this since last night. I thought she might be able to lead us to Peaches."

"Kind of like a Bloodhound," he nodded.

"Yeah, but either she isn't feeling well or something really bad happened to Peaches," Betty continued. "It's almost like she's mourning."

"Well, let's hope not. It was an ugly night last night. The rain was heavy," her husband sighed. "And there's more to come."

"Hey, Reggie. Betty," Morris shouted, jogging up his laneway to catch up to them. "Thought I'd join the search. What with a missing pet and getting kidnapped on yer honeymoon, I figured ya could use the help?"

"Thanks, Morris," Reggie boomed.

"We appreciate it," Betty chimed in. "Where's Brutus and Max?"

"Oh, they're staying with a friend for a couple of days," the goat farmer stammered as he slid to a stop beside them.

Betty and her husband exchanged a look. That was odd. What friend on Seal Island did Morris have who didn't already have a dog? Reggie merely shrugged.

"Gertie sure looks down," Morris noticed.

"She is, that's what's worrying us," Reggie replied.

The three continued down the road, eyes scanning the lots and trees for signs of Peaches. Champ had his nose to the ground. The Border collie circled the three humans and pig, stopping every so often, fixated upon the pig if it didn't keep up.

"Splash, leave Gertie alone," Reggie barked at the collie.

"He's just dying to herd her," Morris reported, a look of admiration on his face. "Nice dog. I heard about him through the grapevine. Strange though. I can't believe a collie would leave its master on the West Coast Trail. You sure these folks coming to get him are for real?"

"They sent us a picture with a dog that looked a lot like him," Betty responded.

"But it was a fuzzy picture, Bets," Reggie scowled. "We should ask them for more photos."

"Yeah, that's a good idea," she agreed. "I was thinking about that last night. I have tons of photos of Champ, Gertie and Peaches."

"You know I've always had a Border collie. My folks usually kept two. Max is all I need to keep track of my goats. I've got forty now. With all the feral sheep and that one wild pack of goats, it can be hard to keep them at home," Morris said. "I wouldn't mind joining ya when those folks come ta pick that collie up. You can never be too careful."

"We might take ya up on that, Morris," the grizzled fisherman nodded.

Gertrude stopped in front of Tammy Smith's old cottage, refusing to budge. She snorted and stomped a foot.

Betty followed the pig's line of sight and saw Brutus's happy face appear in the living room window. Drool dripped down the glass as he pressed his face against it. A Border collie's face popped up beside it, looking comically at them, ears up, eyes following them.

When the Saint Bernard saw Morris, he started barking. His bark was so enormous that it shook the windowpane.

"I thought you said Brutus was staying with a friend," Betty asked the red-faced goat farmer.

"He is," he shrugged, stubbing the ground with a boot toe. "There she be now."

A little girl with long black hair and startling sea-blue eyes looked out the window, one thin arm wrapped around the giant dog, the other around the collie's. Her face was an emotionless mask as she lifted a limp hand and waved at them. There was a flicker of a smile when she laid eyes on Gertrude.

"Who's that? And what is a little girl doing in Tammy's house," Reggie mumbled, perplexed.

"Oh, she and her pa are house sitting for a while," Morris lied. "Seems the lawyer hired them."

Betty rolled her eyes at Morris. She wasn't buying that and would investigate it more later. She had a cow to find. The rain forecasted started to fall. Time was of the essence.

Champ suddenly barked. It wasn't a low bark of warning, but a high-pitched bark that set Betty's nerves on edge.

He wagged his tail, nose to the ground, and then took off like a shot towards the end of the road.

"I think he's scented Peaches," Morris thundered, racing after the shepherd.

Betty and Reggie sprinted after Morris and the German shepherd, the Border collie matching their pace. Gertrude squealed in distress.

"Come on, Gertie, let's go," Betty yelled over her shoulder.

The pig snorted and trotted after them, belly sloshing from side to side like an overstuffed water balloon.

***

The German shepherd galloped around the clearing, nostrils flared, nose to the ground. The Border collie paced circles around the three human searchers.

Gertrude stopped beside Betty, looked her in the eye, tail windmilling at a furious pace, seeming to brighten up. She trotted off towards the weathered cabin.

"What's up with Gertie," Morris gasped, breathless.

"Looks like she's on a mission, don't it," Reggie surmised, his voice wheezy.

"Champ seems to have lost the scent," Betty sighed, one hand on her right side where a muscle stitch almost had her bowling over. She wasn't quite up to jogging in the rain anymore.

"One of us should follow Gertie," Morris suggested. "She may be on to something."

"Let's all go," Reggie agreed. "Champ's clearly lost the scent."

"Champ. Splash," Betty called the dogs. "Heel."

Gertrude's rump was barely visible through the trees. The sod hut was a couple hundred yards from the treasure dig site. The group strode after her, cutting through the trees until they came upon the prophet's forlorn looking cabin.

Immediately, they could see that the roof had caved in. A jagged outline of a broken beam flipped a bird at the sky. Even from a hundred feet away, Betty could see the gaping hole in the roof.

Gertrude snuffled around the front door, clearly agitated. She tried to force her way in, bumping against it with her chest to no avail. She squealed and grunted in dismay, her temper flaring.

A long, low 'mooooo' greeted them.

"That sounds like Peaches," Betty stammered.

"Aye, I think it's coming from inside the cabin," Reggie murmured, his face furrowed in concern.

"Lordie, ya don't think she fell through the roof, do ya," Morris gasped. "I mean that hole looks big enough to fit a cow and I've chased her off of it several times."

Betty, Reggie and Morris bolted for the sod hut, the dogs barking at their heels.

"Bets, there's a fella inside," Reggie cried, pushing the tattered plastic sheeting aside to look through the window. "And he's stuck under Peaches."

"Good lord will ya look at that," Morris added, joining Reggie at the window.

"The door's stuck," Betty hissed, pushing Gertrude aside and trying to shoulder her way through the blocked doorway. "The door is all twisted. Peaches' rear end is shoved up against it."

"Yeah, I can see it from here," Reggie agreed, leaning through the window and looking towards the door. "It doesn't look like her legs are broke. Nothing's cockeyed anyway. If she gets up, she's gonna kill that fella underneath her. He doesn't look so good to me, but he's breathing. I can see his chest rising and falling."

"That's Sam's father," Morris exclaimed. "What's he doing here?"

"Why's he wearing a Santa Claus suit?"

"Well, I reckon he's that Santa thief everyone's been talking about," Morris whispered, a guilty tone in his voice.

"Regardless, how're we going to get them out safely," Betty asked worriedly, once again pushing the worried pig aside.

"I'll call the fire chief," Morris quaked, pulling out his cell phone to call the volunteer fire department.

"Why don't we get Frank over here with some ropes and his tractor," Reggie suggested. "Maybe he can tug that door off."

"Good idea," Betty quaked, her thoughts all jumbled up. *Did Peaches have a broken leg? Would the man on the floor survive if they got her to her feet like Reggie worried about?*

Betty dialed the McDonald's farm.

"Frank," she sobbed into her cell phone. "We're at the prophet's cabin. Peaches and a man are trapped inside. Can you come with some rope or chains and your tractor?"

Betty listened for a moment and then hung up.

"He's on his way," she trembled. She took a deep breath and centered herself. Now was not the time to fall apart, no matter how tough the past few days had been or how exhausted she was.

"Okay, gents, hoist me up so I can get through this window," Betty said, squaring her shoulders. "Santa and Peaches are depending on us. Unless you want to do it, Morris? Reg, honey, you're too tall."

"That's my girl," Reggie whispered into her ear as he cupped his hands into a stirrup, and she stepped into them.

"I'm good," Morris replied, steadying her from behind. "Besides, I need to go make sure Sam doesn't run down here once she sees the fire trucks roll by. I don't want her to see her father like this."

"Good idea, Morris," Betty responded. "Maybe take her down to Pearl's with your dogs. We don't want Brutus and Max to come barreling up here either."

Sirens roared in the distance as the volunteer fire department raced towards them. Trees fell. Stumps were smashed to smithereens. Frank's John Deere tractor cut a wide swath through the forest, chains spinning in the mud, black smoke bellowing out the exhaust pipe, as it made its way towards them.

Betty steeled herself for the worst as she climbed into the cabin. The man pinned beneath the cow was ashen faced. It would be a miracle if he survived.

**

Chris heard voices, lots of voices, men and women alike. His face felt warm. He thought he felt a soft caress across his face, but then remembered the cow leaning over him. Life was filled with disappointments. He prayed that the last touch upon his skin would not be that of a cow's breath.

"Hey, can you hear me," a deep feminine voice whispered in his ear. "If you can, squeeze my fingers."

Was the voice real?

It did feel like someone was holding his hand.

Chris felt drained. He was sure the world was on fire. Pain coursed through his left side. His legs were numb and lifeless. He tried to wiggle a toe but couldn't.

"Do you hear me," the husky voice asked again.

"Yes," he hissed, forcing his numb fingers to close around the warm hand that gripped his.

"He's alive," another person shouted over top of him. This voice was male. The man's form was vaguely visible in the window above his head. He wore a giant hat.

"I'm coming in with a med kit," a younger male voice replied.

A med kit?

Was he hurt?

Of course, he chastised himself, the confusion lifting like a theatre curtain at the start of a Broadway play. *He was on a job, had thought the house was empty, but it wasn't. The mistake had nearly cost him his life. What a fool he was. He wanted to make a big score… and where did it get him. Here! Dying. Under a cow!*

"Looks like he's been shot," the younger man said. "I need to change this dressing on his side. The wound is still leaking."

"Do what you have to," the smokey female voice said with an air of authority. "I'm going to sidle over the other side of him and try to keep Peaches from scrambling to her feet when they get the door open."

Peaches, Chris thought, fighting to stay conscious, *that must be the cow. Wasn't that the name of the pig's buddy? Wasn't the pig and cow friends of his daughter?*

Chris grimaced when the paramedic, or whoever the kid was, ripped his makeshift bandage off the gunshot wound. The stink coming from the wound was nauseating.

Speaking of Sam… was she all right?

"Sam," he moaned. "Where's my daughter?"

Chris started to shiver. He had gone from boiling hot to icy cold in an instant. Tremors wracked his body. Rain fell upon his face.

"Don't worry about your daughter," the woman replied, using her body to shield him. "She's in good hands."

The woman smelled of Irish Spring soap, fried eggs and bacon. It was a delightful smell.

Chris forced his eyes open. It was hard to do. They were caked with sand and debris.

The woman's face hovering over his was round. A halo of light made her silver blond hair look like peach fuzz. Behind her, a black-haired, dark-skinned man dressed in a blue and gold robe stared down at him. The figure was right out of a B grade fantasy movie. He wasn't scary like Mordred from the King Arthur tale. In fact, the man looked deeply concerned for his welfare.

I must be losing it, he thought.

A loud tearing noise shattered the peace of the moment. It sounded like the universe had been ripped in two. The wood rendering ear-splitting screech of a cranky engine followed it.

Light fell upon his face.

The tangy smell of the sea filled the room.

The cow thrashed. A cloven hoof slammed into his chest.

Chris screamed until he lost his breath, and then everything went black.

***

"Hold on to her," Reggie hollered, dashing into the cabin as the tractor hauled away the chain wrapped door.

"I can't," his wife yelled. "She's too strong."

The cow was on its knees, one hoof slamming into the downed man's chest as the firefighter tending to the injured man scrambled out of the way.

Reggie wrapped one arm under the cow's neck and one over its withers. With all his might, he lifted and pulled backwards.

Peaches bellowed and staggered into him, slamming Reggie into the wall.

"Yank him outa there," he screamed at the firefighter while his wife pushed the cow's legs off the man's chest and to the floor.

The firefighter jumped into action, grabbing the red velvet

clad man under the arms and hauling him out from beneath the cow.

"I got him," the firefighter shouted.

"Peaches has to go first before we can enter," the volunteer fire department chief shouted over the drone of the tractor.

Reggie nodded his head as he fought to balance the balking cow.

"I don't think she's hurt, honey, just scared," his wife wailed.

Reggie felt a hand on his shoulder and turned to see Frank McDonald, a steady stream of water dripping off his hat as a raging downpour fell upon the earth. Frank slipped around Reggie and wrapped a lead rope around the cow's neck.

"Come around here, Betty, and take the rope. I'll help Reggie muscle Peaches out the door," Frank rumbled.

Betty grabbed the lead rope and fastened a figure eight loop around Peaches' head and nose while her husband and Frank struggled to pull the cow out of the cabin, away from the two men in the corner.

"Shhh, Peaches, it's okay," Betty whispered to the cow, trying to calm it as they worked to free the trembling beast.

Finally, the Jersey cow's wobbly legs supported its weight. She had a few scrapes and abrasions, but there didn't appear to be any broken bones.

"Let's lead her out of here, Bets," Reggie said through gritted teeth, his chest heaving from the exertion.

"Okay, got it," Betty said, tugging the cow towards the door.

Peaches stumbled forward.

The Jersey cow saw Gertrude and bellowed happily.

The pot-bellied pig raced over to check on her friend as Betty led it out of the building.

"We got it from here," the fire chief said, waving his men into the cabin with their first aid equipment. "The medi-vac chopper will be landing on the beach in the next twenty minutes."

Frank nodded as he exited the cabin alongside Reggie. He grinned and clapped a hand over Reggie's shoulder.

"We did it," the lanky tussle haired farmer sighed.

"We did," Reggie agreed.

Betty unwrapped the lead rope from around the peach colored cow's head and returned to her husband's side. They watched through the doorway as the men worked to save the life of the Santa Claus thief.

"You know, I should have checked here this morning when your dad called me, Betty," the handsome farmer said.

"Why's that," Betty inquired.

"I noticed the catamaran was back in our cove this morning," Frank croaked. "He's been mooring it there this past week or so. Morris asked me to keep an eye on him a few days ago because he was leaving his little girl alone at Tammy Smith's place."

"Unless ya had a crystal ball, Frank, ya couldn't have known that Peaches had gone through the roof and trapped them both inside the Brother's place," Reggie consoled the downcast farmer.

"Yeah, but me and Morris have been chasing people out of here ever since you guys unearthed the Brother's loot last summer," he grumbled. "It just hasn't stopped. I chased Peaches off that roof several times too. Crazy cow."

"Captain Hindsight, Frank," Betty added, glancing towards the pig and cow who were already off on another mission heading towards South Shore Road. "None of us have a cape or a crystal ball."

"True," Frank agreed as the men inside the cabin readied Santa Claus for transport.

Four firefighters carried the unconscious man out of the cabin. For the man's daughter's sake, Betty hoped he would make it.

Home is Where the Heart Is

December 23rd

"What if I don't want to go," Sam whined, tears in her eyes. "Why can't I stay with you or Morris?"

"She's your mother, honey," Pearl hugged the child to her chest. "She's been looking for you for a long time."

"But I don't even know her," the raven-haired girl pleaded, looking from Pearl to Morris and then to Betty who stood on the landing in front of the docks to see the girl off.

"No, but you will," the old woman consoled the girl.

"Please, Betty, let me stay here," she cried.

"Sweetie, she's your mum," Betty responded. "Give her a chance."

"I'm sure she'll let you come visit," Morris added, standing uncomfortably beside Pearl, Brutus and Mazie sitting patiently together on either side of them. Max rested on the ground at his feet.

"But what if she doesn't and what if she won't let me visit my daddy either?" she wailed.

"My friend Sam, don't cry," Also croaked, his voice not quite recovered yet.

Sam looked into the beautiful, earnest face of her best friend in all the world. His raspberry beret was cocked at a jaunty angle to the right of center. A black topcoat that was far too big for him flowed almost to the ground. His cheeks were the same color as his hat.

Also's auntie had allowed Also to see her off provided he came right back home with Morris afterwards.

The ferry pulled in and a middle-aged long-haired brunette in a bright yellow ski jacket, jeans, and black leather boots climbed off it. She wore a raspberry beret that was almost the same as Also's, except it had a pompom sewn on the top. The ferry man handed her a travel suitcase, which she gracefully accepted.

Reggie stood on the deck of *The Persephone,* moored across from the ferry dock, dressed in an off-white cable-knit sweater and grey toque, his ball bearing grey beard neatly trimmed. Beside Reggie sat Champ, the once fearful German shepherd, and the Border collie named Splash who once was lost, but now was found. The collie had growled at the people who came to pick it up and refused to leave the Phoenix's boat. Morris and a few other fishermen had escorted the couple back to their boat, informing them in no uncertain terms to never return to Seal Island. Both the shepherd and the collie watched the woman disembark off the ferry. Today, she was the lone passenger.

"Look, your mom has a hat just like mine," Also clapped.

"Why does she have a suitcase," Sam asked, looking up at the grownups forming a semi-circle around her.

"We'll have to ask her," Pearl shrugged.

The woman took one look at the odd assortment of people gathered on the dock, zeroed in on Sam, dropped the suitcase, and raced across the dock, hair streaming out behind her, tears in her eyes. She collapsed on one knee in front of Sam.

"Oh, my God, I had given up hope," Sam's mother cried. "I thought I'd never see you again. I've been looking for you for six years."

Sam took a step back, not sure what to make of this emotional woman who claimed to be her mother. She supposed she looked a little familiar, though. There was something about the woman's nose and mouth that reminded Sam of her own reflection in the mirror.

"Knock. Knock," Also beamed.

"Okay, I'll bite," the teary-eyed woman grinned. "Who's there?"

"Boo," Sam's friend grinned.

"Boo who," Sam's mother sniffled, drying her eyes with a well-worn tissue.

"Hey, don't cry," Also giggled, wrapping one arm over her shoulder.

The group on the landing chuckled.

"I like your hat," Also said, pulling away and pointing at the woman's beret.

"I like yours too," Shelly Nicholas replied.

"Mrs Nicholas, I'm Betty Phoenix," Betty said, stepping forward to introduce yourself. "We talked on the phone."

"Thank you so much for calling me directly, Mrs Phoenix," Shelly chattered away. "I really can't thank you enough for everything you've done for us. For me and Sam, I mean. You have all been so kind."

Sam realized with a start that her mother seemed as worried about their meeting as she was. That made her feel a little better.

Reggie jumped down to the wharf and grabbed the woman's wheeled suitcase. He tucked it under one arm and sauntered down the dock, the shepherd and collie jogging ahead of him.

"I think ya forgot this," the old fisherman chortled, handing Sam's mother her bag.

"Oh gosh, thank you," she gushed, taking the bag from his hand.

"Yer lucky it didn't fall in the salt chuck," he laughed merrily.

"What's the bag for," Sam asked sheepishly.

"Well, I didn't want to pull you away from your friends at Christmas so I rented a two-bedroom cabin beside the marina so we can get to know each other," Shelly confessed, her face reddening. "I thought we'd spend Christmas here. That's okay, isn't it?"

"I've got Christmas dinner all organized," Pearl rejoiced. "Why do you think I had you help me with all that extra baking over the past few days, Sam? It's going to be a big one. I'm too old to do dinner for twelve all by myself."

"Really? We're not going to rush off on the ferry," Sam squeaked, her voice warbling.

"No, baby, we're not," her mother replied, opening her arms

for a hug.

Sam didn't know what to say. Maybe it wasn't going to be so bad after all.

"My friend Sam," Also whispered in her ear. "I think your mama is waiting for a hug. You can't never have too many hugs."

Sam grinned and flew into her mother's arm. The woman kneeling in front of her smelled of flowers and cinnamon. The scent triggered a memory of sparkling lights, a beautiful Christmas tree, heaps of colorfully wrapped presents beneath it, and the hiss of flickering candles.

Joy filled Sam's heart. She looked from one person to the other and saw the delight in their eyes. The dogs took advantage of the opportunity and knocked Sam and her mother flying, Saint Bernard spit flying in every direction.

Too late, everyone realized that Gertrude and Peaches had shown also up for the occasion.

Pandemonium erupted as Sam and her mother howled with laughter as they were assaulted by animals on all sides.

The End
I hope you enjoyed this novel, the last book in this series.
I always felt that five was my magic number.
Please consider leaving an honest review on Amazon,
Bookbub or Goodreads.

It only takes a minute of your time to leave a review and
it means a lot to the author and their family.

Happy holidays.
Peace and wellness to all.

To learn about upcoming releases, simply hit the "follow
me" button on: www.Running L Productions

Novels by Laura Hesse

The Unicorn Daze Series (children's fantasy):
Gus, The Flood, The Unicorn King, The Unicorn & The Dragon, The King of Christmas, The Unicorn Wears Red

The Holiday Series (children/family equine series):
One Frosty Christmas, The Great Pumpkin Ride, A Filly Called Easter, Independence, Valentino

Paranormal Thriller:
The Thin Line of Reason

The Gumboot & Gumshoe Series:
Book One: Gumboots, Gumshoes & Murder
Book Two: The Dastardly Mr. Deeds
Book Three: Murder Most Fowl
Book Four: Gertrude & The Sorcerer's Gold
Book Five: Chasing Santa

Non-fiction/Adventure & Comedy/Western:
The Silver Spurs Home for Aging Cowgirls
Peter Pan Wears Steel Toes

If you want to find out more about Laura Hesse or hear about her upcoming releases, then visit www.RunningLProductions.com

About The Author

Laura Hesse

Laura lives on Vancouver Island with a rescue dog and two old cats. She grew up a backstage brat in Music Hall Theatre and credits her mother with her love of song and theatre.

Laura spent many happy years riding the trails and writes about the special horses in her life within the pages of her children's and young adult series of equine novels. While Pumpkin Sally and all the rest have passed over the rainbow, they will forever live on in her stories.

www.ingramcontent.com/pod-product-compliance
Lightning Source LLC
Chambersburg PA
CBHW070502260626
47161CB00004B/1414